Banner Peak (photo by author)

Married a Hiker, Got a Cowboy

A Memoir

NANCY W. BROWN

iUniverse®

MARRIED A HIKER, GOT A COWBOY
A MEMOIR

iUniverse books may be ordered through booksellers or by contacting:

iUniverse
1663 Liberty Drive
Bloomington, IN 47403
www.iuniverse.com
1-800-Authors (1-800-288-4677)

ISBN: 978-1-5320-6874-4 (sc)
ISBN: 978-1-5320-6875-1 (e)

Library of Congress Control Number: 2019902467

Print information available on the last page.

iUniverse rev. date: 11/08/2019

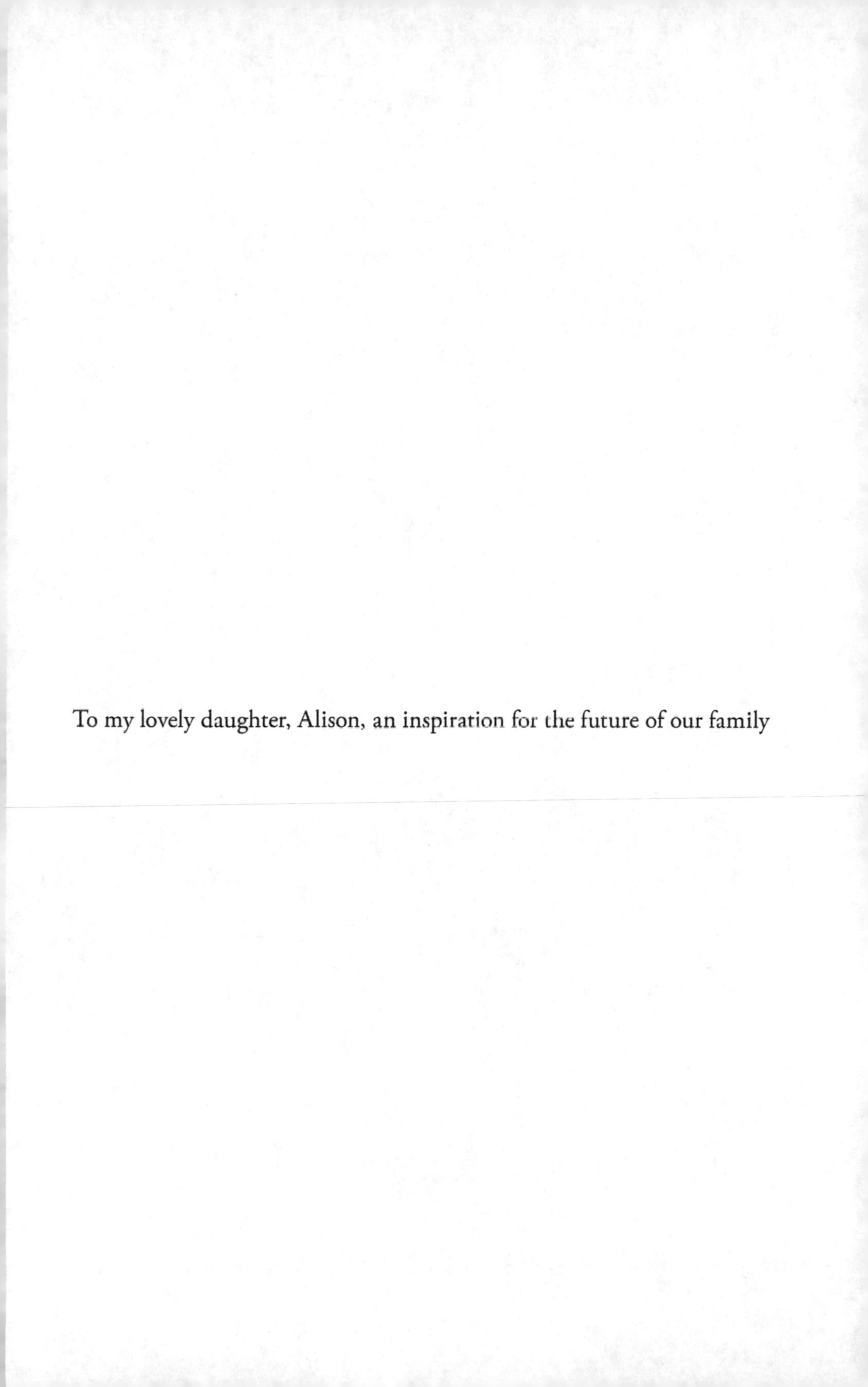

To my lovely daughter, Alison, an inspiration for the future of our family

To my lovely daughter, Alison, an inspiration for the future of our family

Preface

Grandma Nellie and I were sitting on her rustic back porch, shelling peas, one summer when I was eight. We sat in dappled light, overlooking the apple orchard, and I was feeling happy that I was visiting my grandparents for a week. I proudly announced that I was going to "write a book" and asked whether I could please have some paper.

She sharply replied, "You can't do that! You're too young to write a book!"

I suddenly felt hurt and homesick, but I don't recall ever telling my mother what had happened. I know she would have given me a ream of paper if I had asked. She loved reading and started a book herself when she was young. Now I wish she and my father were here to see this book that I have finally completed at age seventy-five. Like my parents, I have loved books all my life, and it's been a satisfying experience to create one myself.

I lived my adventurous life and never again had much time or desire to write until a few years ago when I realized I had a unique story to share, particularly for my family and closest friends. By this time, my life seemed like a trail with several forks and intersections that I wanted to recall—a childhood plus three adventurous marriages that could become a memoir, perhaps as much for myself as for anyone else.

Looking back, I have healed from disappointments and developed understanding of things that only time and the creative, contemplative process could bring me. This story has been written almost entirely from my memory with the exception of a few scratchy travel journals, historical details, and dates. If there is one theme in my life, it would be my outdoor adventures and where they have carried me over the years.

So take the first step with me and begin the journey. Climb mountains; cross passes; raise a talented, adventurous daughter; paddle rivers; and ride a mule. I have enjoyed recalling this life and am now happy to pass on the story to my grandchildren. May they follow in my footsteps and continue our family tradition of seeking wilderness places that soothe the soul and enhance their lives.

CHAPTER 1

Up and at 'Em

When I was a child, it always seemed odd that my parents had been married in a cemetery. I later learned that their wedding had taken place on August 3, 1937, in a small beautiful chapel called Wee Kirk o' the Heather at Forest Lawn Cemetery in Glendale, California. The chapel is a reproduction of a fourteenth-century Scottish church. As an adult, I visited and entered the ivy-covered church through a small enclosed terrace into an intimate chapel with stained glass windows. Then I could see why they chose the place for their wedding, and knowing them, I understood why they chose to do something unusual.

Forest Lawn Cemetery has a parklike setting with acres of trees, flower-adorned chapels, birds singing, and flat brass plaques marking the graves in the acres of mowed grass. Today my mother's grandparents are buried alongside their son Howard, who died of TB before my mother was born. After I visited and quizzed my mother about why she was married there, and why a cemetery, she said she had fond memories of visiting her uncle's grave with her favorite grandmother when she was young. I could now understand as I viewed the flowers cascading off the chapels and heard the birds singing. Forest Lawn is a restful, cheerful, contemplative place, a place for beginnings and endings.

Long before I was born, old family records show that my ancestors on both sides of my family came from England to the Massachusetts area in the early 1600s. They settled in the colonies and gradually moved west to Pennsylvania where, eventually, my grandparents were born. My mother's parents were from Wilkes-Barre, in the northeastern part of the state, an area known for coal mines and lumber. My grandfather Clarence Asa Marcy was born on July 20, 1884, into a family that worked in carpentry and the lumber industry. His grandfather had been killed in a logging accident when a log jumped out of a logging chute. His father, my great-grandfather Orlondo B. (OB) Marcy, however, was still living and visiting us in Northern California when I was a baby in the 1940s. My great-grandmother Irena R. Marcy had died in 1933.

My mother's father, Clarence, received his teaching certificate and started his first teaching job at age seventeen in a normal school in the lumber community. Some of the kids who were bigger than he was ganged up on him and shoved him out the window because he was the new inexperienced teacher. He would later become a tall strapping man himself, but that was a tough way to start out. Eventually, he and his younger brother, Howard, would leave the area, working their way west by train to California, selling *The World Book of Knowledge* throughout the Pacific Northwest, down through Washington and Oregon, and arriving in Los Angeles in 1904. There they felt they had found the promised land and would send boxes of fruit back to the family in Pennsylvania. Clarence would eventually return to Pennsylvania to marry his childhood sweetheart, Nellie Fine, on June 28, 1911, and bring her back to California. His brother, Howard N. Marcy, died June 25, 1919, in a TB sanatorium in Banning, California.

In 1910, my great-grandparents also moved to Los Angeles and eventually settled in Fullerton, California, in 1920. My mother often told the story of her grandmother following behind the mule-drawn vegetable and milk wagons, scooping up the manure for her garden. Great-grandma used to spend her time in the garden and feed her husband his plain boiled vegetables. He didn't like casseroles—referred to them as "too much of that mixed-up stuff!" Years later, I visited their modest home when I was very young, and I still remember the pretty garden and goldfish pond crossed by a little arched bridge.

My grandfather Clarence, a respected science teacher in areas of Los Angeles—Fillmore, Fullerton, Manhattan Beach—eventually became superintendent of schools. In addition to his teaching, he was a well-known naturalist and photographer who led weekend nature trips into the surrounding areas. As a child, I was very impressed with his stories and old photographs. I still have his books and cameras, his hand-tinted glass lantern slides and old projector, and a plant press that he used for his collection of wildflowers. Los Angeles in the early 1900s was bordered with rural areas to explore. His knowledge and interest in the natural world remain a theme in our family to this day.

My mother, Ferne Marcy Williams, was born July 25, 1913, in Fillmore, California, the oldest of three girls. All three, Ferne, Dawn, and Margaret, became socially grounded and artistic. Being the oldest, my mother was encouraged to be very responsible; her mother expected her to cook, clean, and babysit, as well as advance in school and music. My grandfather placed a small cast-iron owl on her desk to keep his eye on her and encourage her to be a "wise owl." She excelled academically in high school and even did the artwork for one of her father's school textbooks called *The Indians' Garden*, on California Indians, when she was only eighteen.

My father's parents were from Pittsburgh, Pennsylvania, where my grandfather Albert D. Williams, born June 14, 1883, eventually became a businessman. As an office boy, he had shown promise at working with numbers and steadily advanced in the General Cable Company, which would eventually provide cables for the construction of the Golden Gate Bridge in 1937. Ultimately, that brought Albert and his family to the Bay Area, where he continued his career with the cable company. He remained a businessman all his life. When he retired, he would buy a new car each year and show it off when we visited, and he would also slip my brother and me each a fifty-cent piece and tell us to put it in the bank.

My father, Edward Augustus Williams, was born in Pittsburgh, Pennsylvania, on February 16, 1914. He had a sister, Arlene, who was four years older, and eventually a brother, Albie, two years younger. When my father was four, his mother, Effie (Sherrer), died from pneumonia. Too young to understand grieving, he was severely punished when he bounced down the stairs, saying, "My mother is dead. My mother is dead." After their mother's death, he and his siblings were put in the care of relatives until my grandfather married Effie's sister Cordelia in 1921. That marriage produced another child, Carol, my father's half- sister. In all, there were four children.

My father's memories in Pittsburgh were of playing with his cousins, sledding in the snow, ice-skating, and the smell of coal burning in the fireplace. He spoke fondly of his aunts and uncles who cared for him after his mother died, but he never spoke fondly of his stepmother, Cordelia. One can imagine how difficult her role may have been taking on the care of her sister's three children, but my aunt Arlene said in later years that Cordelia was particularly cruel to my father and even burned his hands once with a hot iron. Nevertheless, when I was a child, we socialized on holidays and visited them at their rural home in Alamo, California, where they had beautiful property with a walnut orchard and a view of Mount Diablo.

When my father and his brother were in high school, the family moved to California. To begin the school year, my father and his brother came ahead of the family via the Panama Canal on a banana boat with the United Fruit Company. Thereafter, my father never liked bananas because of seasickness he'd endured after eating them on board. After arrival in San Francisco, both boys stayed with friends in Oakland until the family arrived. My father always told the story of being called "the Duke" by the kids at Oakland Technical High School when he enrolled in his eastern attire of knickers, shirt, and tie. When the family arrived, they settled first in Oakland and then Berkeley. Eventually, all four children attended the University of California, Berkeley, and lived together with their parents in a rented house in North Berkeley on Vine Street. By this time, my mother and her sister, Dawn, were both attending UC and renting an apartment together in Berkeley. Later, my mother would meet my father in the kitchen of the Vine Street house where she did cooking and light housekeeping for the family as she worked to supplement her college expenses. Apparently, my father walked through the kitchen door, and they were mutually attracted to each other from the beginning.

My mother was smartly dressed and beautiful, with her fair skin and wavy auburn hair. My dad was handsome, not quite six feet, and slender and had a quick smile and sense of humor. Stories of their early dates had them going by ferry to San Francisco and racing back to the dock, barely catching the boat to get back to the East Bay. They enjoyed smoking, drinking, dancing, and living the good life of college students in the 1930s. They had each been raised strictly and traditionally, in churchgoing families, and now was the time to kick up their heels. They were artistic and fun-loving and more liberal than their parents.

Both of my parents and their siblings graduated from UC Berkeley. My mother had studied English and art, and my dad landscape architecture. My father graduated in December 1935, followed by my mother in May 1936. A year later, they were married in Southern California, where my mother's family still lived. The wedding at Forest Lawn was attended by twenty-five relatives and friends. There were three attendants—Dawn Marcy, Albert Williams Jr., and a close college friend, Alden McClelland. My mother made her own wedding dress of soft light pink taffeta, but the lace veil is the only part that I still have. I have never seen any photographs of the wedding day, which is surprising since my grandfather was such a good photographer.

After their wedding, my parents had a two-week honeymoon at Big Bear Lake in the San Gregorio Mountains where Clarence had built a cabin when my mother was young and where she had spent all her summer days swimming, canoeing, and exploring. Her father had given her a bright red Old Town canoe when she had learned to swim to the small island offshore. My parents enjoyed paddling that canoe during their honeymoon, and many years later, we still took it on camping trips on top of the woody station wagon when I was growing up.

After the honeymoon, my parents settled in the Bay Area, first in San Francisco in an apartment on Nob Hill. My father began his career in landscape architecture at this time, and my mother worked at the City of Paris department store downtown. As was the custom then, she wore a dress, hat, and gloves every day when riding public transportation to work. After living in San Francisco, they moved to Palo Alto, where they rented a small house on Oberlin Street in College Terrace near Stanford University. After my brother Lauren (Larry) Marcy Williams was born on January 15, 1941, they moved to Hunters Point, where they lived near the waterfront. Hunters Point in those days was quiet, scenic, and quaint. Their next rental was a house in Redwood City, but when they became tired of renting, they eventually bought their first house. Throughout their lives together, they would become a creative team that balanced work with family home life and outdoor vacations.

As a result of this background, when my brother and I came along, we grew up exposed to the idea that life would be fulfilling if we were creative, well read, and well educated and spent many hours in the out-of-doors.

My mother, Ferne, was always a homemaker, seamstress, and excellent cook, as well as a gardener. She knew plants—both wildflowers and domestic species. She was also a good writer and started a book about the first house my parents owned and remodeled. In my early years, she did watercolor painting, taking Larry, me, and her easel into the countryside near Redwood City where she painted. In later years, she made and sold stone and silver jewelry created at home in her own lapidary shop. She kept a huge collection of handwritten recipes that I still have today, and she could throw a beautiful dinner party for friends and my dad's colleagues. The warm family home always looked clean and was creatively and comfortably furnished. She balanced homemaking with her own artistic pursuits, as well as being a very supportive wife and mother. There were frustrations too as she helped my father through years of business conflicts and challenges that were to come.

When I was growing up, my father, Edward (Ed), was becoming a well-known landscape architect. After his graduation from UC Berkeley, he partnered with my uncle Garrett Eckbo in 1939. Garrett had studied at UC Berkeley with him and was married to my father's sister, Arlene. Over the years, others came and left the partnership, and eventually the firm became known as Eckbo, Dean, Austin and Williams, but known today as EDAW, Inc. and still in San Francisco. In the early days, when I was growing up, the firm designed gardens for private homes and businesses in the San Francisco Bay Area, such as the Firemen's Fund, Chevron Oil Refinery, Southland Mall, St. Mary's Square, Stanford Research Institute, and later in 1965, one of his favorites, the Garden of Fragrance for the blind and handicapped in Golden Gate Park. Then in my early adulthood, he did land-use study for the states of California and Hawaii. From then on, EDAW grew into a larger landscape and urban planning firm with related offices all over the country. At home, my dad always had remodeling or gardening projects and lots of cheerful energy for accomplishing things. I always enjoyed his positive attitude. He called me "Toots" and "Nance" with affection. He and my mother worked well together planning and finishing projects—mostly with their own elbow grease.

World War II was in full swing when I was born on March 20, 1943, at Mills Memorial Hospital in Redwood City, California. My first and middle names, Nancy Carol, were not chosen because of any prior family connection. My birth went smoothly, but I had to return to the hospital with pneumonia when I was eighteen months, and I had an allergic reaction to penicillin. In those days, parents couldn't stay with children in the hospital, and my mom later told me that she heard me screaming all the way down the hallway when she had to leave.

My brother Larry was two, and my parents were both thirty when I was born. My dad was doing design work in the Hunters Point shipyards during the war. I came home from the hospital to the small house my parents were remodeling from the time they bought it until we moved away several years later. I lived there until I was seven, so I can remember a lot about it even now. The house was at 838 Hillcrest Drive in the Redwood City hills. I still have my mom's typed manuscript, a rough draft, about the house experience. They had become tired of renting and always moving, so they found a house that was not much more than a "shack with possibilities" on a large sloped lot that overlooked a grassy valley; it cost $2,000 at the time.

Today that valley is completely filled with homes, but back then there were only a few neighbors—particularly one I remember who had a horse, caged rabbits, and chickens running around. I revisited the house in 2008 with my daughter and her husband when it was empty and for sale. It was an emotional experience to see it again, especially since it had not changed much in over fifty years. It still had the tall living room windows, some of my dad's built-in bookshelves, and the bedrooms that had been added by my parents and great-grandfather. It was, however, by this time completely surrounded by other homes and was for sale for more than $800,000.

Back in the 1940s, family pictures show Larry and me always among lumber, bare studs, and projects as our parents turned the place into a small home with a nice deck and garden. In my memory, I still smell the sweet alyssum flowers along the brick walkway downhill from the garage. On the west property line, my father planted a long line of poplar trees, and I can remember watering them with my mom when I was old enough to help. They were towering over the house when I returned several years later.

When my mother was pregnant with me, her grandfather Orlondo B. Marcy, born April 13, 1859, would come from Los Angeles to help with the construction. He didn't like being far from my brother, his only great-grandson, and agreed to come north by train even though he felt the Bay Area was "a den of iniquity where unions thrive and are a threat to the free man." "Grampa" was seventy-eight, but was still a capable carpenter and woodworker. He would visit again the next year, and my mom used to tell me that he liked to work in my room during my naps when I was in my crib and would keep me awake tempting me to take the hammer out of his back pocket.

Normally he liked working alone, but he loved having my toddler brother alongside while he worked. My mother wrote, "I could hear them all day long, Larry chirping and pattering about, while Grampa trudged around sawing and hammering and usually singing off key 'Rock of Ages' or another of the good old solid hymns." My parents used to tell the story of how he dragged a huge beam down the hill from the parking area above when they were in town, but he would only say, "Hee, hee, hee," when they asked him how he accomplished that!

Among all this construction, my mom always planted a vegetable garden and morning glories that grew outside the kitchen window. When we were older, we had a sandbox where we spent hours playing with the background sounds of saws and hammers. We had no television or electronic devices in those days, and we played all the time.

Since those early years were influenced by WWII, I am told we had black-out curtains covering the large floor-to-ceiling windows during the period when the west coast of California worried about possible bombings by Japan. My parents had Japanese friends and colleagues who were rounded up and sent to internment camps. Postwar, we visited the Hanamoto family at their pear ranch in central California where we watched them packing the beautiful pears carefully in tissue paper. Asa Hanamoto was a landscape architect who worked with my dad for many years after. They were close family friends who also were on several family fishing trips to Hat Creek in Northern California.

At home, as we grew, we spent much of our time outdoors, playing with other children and watching our neighbor Mr. Burdett care for his rabbits and chickens, even witnessing him kill them for food. He chopped chickens' heads off on a chopping block and skinned rabbits right in front of us. We came to see that as normal, though scary at first. Once when the rabbit cages were empty, Larry locked me in one and walked away, leaving me crying until he returned. Another time, he was using a rake to get a swing out of a tree; I was standing in the wrong place below and got whopped in the head with the rake, which caused a gash in the back of my head that required stitches. I was probably about four or five at the time, but I still remember my mom washing my head in the sink and rushing me to the doctor who shaved the back of my head and stitched me up. I was learning that being a little sister was sometimes hazardous, though most of the time we had fun together.

In our yard, Larry enjoyed digging army-like foxholes in the dirt and playing with model army jeeps. We often played war or cowboy games. I had my own cowgirl hat, chaps, and holster with cap guns. I joined in the dirt play and always loved playing with the little trucks and jeeps, though I loved my dolls as well, and I still have the small pink wooden doll cradle that my dad made for me.

During the war, my parents needed ration stamps for gasoline and could only drive to town once a week. My father walked to and from the bus station while my mother stayed at home, growing vegetables and caring for the home and us. Even the diaper delivery truck could no longer use the gas to reach our house, but delivered to a neighbor downhill where my father would drop off and pick up the diapers. Finally, after the war we could get enough gas to go camping over the hill at Big Basin Redwoods State Park. My parents were so happy to get away from house projects, we went for a week and stayed eleven days. I was told that I took my first "hike" there at age two and was a "good little hiker." During those early years, we started taking many trips to the redwoods and county beaches. It was about this time that my parents decided to spend some time getting away instead of working continuously on the house.

I have an early recollection of my room with colorful curtains my mom had made and a record player with a needle that stuck on "Jack and Jill went up the hill to fetch a pail of water, water, water." When I was little, my mom said she had to move my playpen away from the bookcases to prevent me from climbing—possibly my first mountain ascents. When I was preschool age, my brother and I attended a progressive private school, Peninsula School in Menlo Park, he for first and second grades, and I for nursery school and kindergarten. Our mom was the clay teacher there, which must have helped with the private school fees, but apparently I was having separation problems and wanted to go see her in her studio too often. My early report card said I was a sensitive child, but a leader as well. I am still like that today. At Peninsula School, I remember climbing on the jungle gym, napping with hanging blankets between cots in the classroom, and being terrified by a salamander that appeared in the toilet one day, apparently finding its way through the plumbing. Larry remembers the wood shop where he did his first building, and I have a photograph of myself with a hammer and nails. Larry also recalls that one day he decided he would walk home to Redwood City about ten miles away. Luckily, a parent spotted him near the school and brought him back. When Larry and I drove by in 2014, the school was still open, and we recognized the school grounds with the old Victorian house and other buildings, all among beautiful, large oak trees for climbing or perching with a book.

When Larry was ready for third grade, and I for first, we went to public school in Redwood City. Each morning we waited at the corner for a school bus, but when I told my mom there was another mother there teaching us Bible stories with a colorful felt board and characters, my mom was furious and marched down to the bus stop with us the next morning and told the gal to stop. I was upset and cried at bedtime because we didn't "believe in God" and I didn't want to be different. It felt as if we were different from others we met. I realize now that my parents were very liberal for their day. They had friends who had socialist leanings, they knew several Jewish people, and they had befriended a black couple who was being threatened when they moved into a Redwood City neighborhood. My father and other men took turns watching their home at night after whites had burned a cross in their lawn. During this time, my parents also invited the same couple to our home, and I got to hold their tiny baby.

When I was seven, and Larry nine, my parents were tired of remodeling and wanted a more liberal community, so we moved north to Marin County and rented a large old brown shingle house in San Anselmo up the hill on Oak Street. The house came with cats that our kitty Rusty did not like, so he ran away, never to be found again. This wonderful old house was surrounded by large oak trees, huge hydrangea plants, and delightful outdoor play areas. There was an old arbor with wisteria over a fountain and a goldfish pond. The house also came with a family of skunks that had to be caught and removed from under the house by "the skunk lady," a gal who had a trapping business in Marin County. That miserable day, the smell was so bad, I went to my room and put my head under the pillow while she trapped them. Otherwise, the big old house was fun.

There was a long wooden banister to slide down until the day we popped off the decorative ball at the bottom. The upstairs had old pedestal sinks, woodwork trim, and a screened sleeping porch. Outside there were many deer grazing and hiding among the tall shrubs. One day I was naughty and walked all the way home up the hill from school when my mom was late picking me up. It started to rain, and when she got home, she was mad and worried. As I neared the house, I was scared by the deer hiding in the large hydrangea bushes, but I remember feeling I was a brave eight-year-old to walk home from school alone.

Larry and I often played with kids in the big quarry nearby. It was a deep stone quarry where we spent hours climbing and exploring. Most of our playtime was spent running around the hillside neighborhood that was wooded with bay trees, oaks, and redwoods. One April Fools' Day in the old green kitchen, our mom played a practical joke on us, saying the skunks had returned to the backyard and we should tiptoe to peek out the screen door. There were no skunks, just her saying, "April Fools!"

After one year in the rented house in San Anselmo, we moved to Mill Valley where my parents bought a house at 200 Ricardo Road, in the Strawberry area. This was a complete change—a two-story, modern tract house that cost $12,000. The neighborhood had wide streets and sidewalks, but nearby there were still open fields where we played. The yard was barren, but over time, my parents fenced, laid concrete patios, and landscaped it completely. I always loved gardening with them, working in the soil and making things look good. In this way, I grew to love designing and planting gardens myself.

Growing up in Strawberry was wonderful in those days. Lots of freedom and lots of room to play out of doors, either in the rolling hills or at home where we had fun building tepees, log cabins, and forts with the big redwood grape stakes our parents purchased for us. A few years later, in our early teens, a swimming pool was added. Neighbors complained, rightly so, that we were blasting the neighborhood with loud music by Elvis Presley when our parents weren't home. From then on, we couldn't use the radio and extension cord outside.

After moving to Strawberry, I was enrolled in third grade, and Larry in fifth, at Alto School west of Highway 101, which was then a two-lane highway with a stoplight. (We could push our bikes across when we were a little older.) I was miserable in school until I made friends. Every night, I sat in the kitchen, begging to stay home, but my mom insisted that I go. She conferenced with my kind teacher, and within a few weeks, I adjusted when Suzy Rosse stepped forward on the playground, saying, "I'll be your friend!"

My mom became the Campfire Girl leader and had good ideas for activities. One was a puppet show to the music of *Peter and the Wolf* for which we made our own handmade puppets of papier-mâché around light bulbs. Suzy was the cat, I was the duck, and all the other girls had roles as well. From then on, Suzy and I were lifelong friends and still are today. When we wanted to play, we would meet at "the tree," a big eucalyptus tree halfway between our houses. We also sewed and played for hours with Ginny dolls, which were popular small six-inch dolls at that time. My granddaughters Eliza and Jada still play with some of the doll clothes we sewed then. I had many Sunday afternoon dinners with Suzy's family (four kids and a black cocker spaniel) and her friendly parents, who were from Massachusetts. Her dad was an architect, my dad, a landscape architect, and both worked in San Francisco. Her mom worked part-time with her dad, but had graduated from MIT where Suzy's grandfather was dean of men. At their house, there was a huge willow tree and treehouse in the backyard. Suzy and I helped to hang lots of laundry on the line. We were free to wander all over Strawberry area with no fear in those days. We had big groups of neighborhood kids to play with on weekends and after school—games, sliding down grassy slopes on cardboard, wading in puddles, riding bikes, swimming in "the pond," catching frogs, and running with our dogs off leash. Larry built his first rafts at the pond and the bay nearby. We spent many hours out-of-doors on Strawberry Point, which was all grassland then.

When Larry and I were still pretty young, we got a puppy named Muffy, a Sheltie mix that we carried up the hill from a neighbor "to see if your parents like her." Lucky for us, they did, and Muffy was our constant companion growing up, but she was very protective and ferocious with the garbageman, and she broke through the glass front door after the milkman one day. She was so attached to us all that if she stayed in a kennel, she nearly died of a broken heart. She went on almost every family camping trip and even with our parents after we were grown. One night she swallowed a fishhook, and my parents had to drive halfway across Oregon from their campsite to get the hook removed from her esophagus. Years later when I left home to get married, I cried when I said goodbye to Muffy. She lived to be fourteen years old and died after Larry and I both grew up and moved away. Losing her was hard when I learned of it in a letter from home. My mom said later that my dad cried in his leather chair, saying, "The kids have grown, and the dog has died."

My family vacations were always camping trips. My dad would walk through the house, calling, "Up and at 'em!" waking us at four in the morning to get on the road. My parents always packed the car the previous night to make an early start for the long drives. They loaded us into the car, still in pajamas, with pillows and blankets, and we would sleep until the sun came up. I remember singing with our parents, learning "You Are My Sunshine," "Bicycle Built for Two," and "Irene, Good Night." We would also look for geographical landmarks or notable trees such as a very large "monkey puzzle tree" in Santa Rosa that my dad would always point out after he built up the suspense as we approached. Early camping trips were to the Big Basin Redwoods, the San Mateo Beaches, but later we ventured to Hat Creek in Northern California, as well as many rivers and lakes wherever my parents could fish. My mother, Ferne, was an excellent outdoors woman. Growing up, she had spent every summer at Big Bear Lake playing out of doors, collecting wildflowers, canoeing, and swimming. She learned to fish with her father, and when I was young, she had her own split bamboo fly rod and tied her own flies. I still have her old fly rod and some of her handtied flies.

My father, Ed, had not grown up camping, but he had a good sense of adventure and learned fast. I loved his story of descending Tioga Pass once with his brother in a Model A-Ford and having to stand on the brakes going downhill. He was a good hiker, an excellent swimmer, and excelled in sports at UC Berkeley. As it turned out, he loved camping and always enjoyed setting up a good camp in the mountains.

In the winter of 1950, our family took a camping trip to Death Valley National Monument (now Park). Just the name was enough to scare me at age seven, and I didn't want to go. (Luckily, no one gave in to my objections, and I have been going ever since, for more than sixty-five years.) We went with family friends and camped at various sites. I remember camping at Bennett Wells. It must have been a moonlit night because I have a distinct memory of seeing the shadows of wild burros on our white canvas tent and hearing coyotes at night. Today, camping is not allowed along the West Side Road at those historic sites, but it was then, and I have photos of us standing near the old chimney of Eagle Borax Works. I am sure that my love of burros (donkeys) began then, because the wild burros were not totally shy and would wander nearby. Now they have been removed from the park, deemed to be a threat to the bighorn sheep who are indigenous. The burros were all offspring from the prospectors' pack animals. Also on that trip, we rode the little tourist train at Ryan, the old mining town east of Furnace Creek. That train no longer runs, but in those days, it was a popular tourist activity. We also visited Scotty's Castle, where my brother and I remember meeting Scotty himself—an old character with a huge hat, entertaining visitors with his long, drawn-out stories. Also, we visited Rhyolite and the famous bottle house built of AB beer bottles on their sides and cemented together. We met the builder, Tom, who is long-gone today, but the story lives on with the recent restoration of the house and grounds. I have visited it many times over the years.

On another adventure, when I was about ten, we took a backpack trip into the Desolation Valley Wilderness and camped by a lake at about eight-thousand-feet elevation. Because we had come from sea level and were not acclimated, the hike was tough on everyone, and I got my first altitude sickness. My parents never backpacked again because they preferred car camping, but I took it up again in my early twenties, covered many miles, and never stopped until I was about sixty.

Since my parents loved to fish, one summer we went to the Caribou Lakes in the Trinity Alps in Northern California on a horse pack trip. We drove all the way into Coffee Creek in the family woody station wagon, and then we were packed in about ten miles to the lakes by the packer Nate Steele. As young as I was, I think I fell in love with that cowboy who led me on my first trail ride. I felt very sad when we were left there to camp alone without the cowboy and horses, but I got over it, especially when I caught my first fish. It was cold at night, though, and our wool sleeping bags were not warm enough. Larry and I froze in our little army pup tent, but our mom's cooking was great—breakfasts with eggs, spam or bacon, and pancakes; dinners of corned beef hash and eggs, or hot dogs and beans, all good camp food. Our parents always set up a great camp. Campfires were always allowed in those days, and we often cooked over the fire. I still have, and use, the long forks with wooden handles that we had for roasting hot dogs or marshmallows. Those forks must be seventy years old now.

In addition to camping trips, for a while we owned a very rustic unfinished cabin on Maacama Creek in Sonoma County. It's not surprising that my mother would be eager for such an adventure after her upbringing, and my dad loved to build and always had a good vision for remodeling. Our Maacama Creek cabin was rough, with no running water or plumbing, and it had unfinished interior walls. We had an outhouse covered with moss and lichens. The interior of the cabin was creepy at night even though my parents would set up cots and cozy bedding, but the bats would come out at night and terrify me.

During the day, the place was fun. Larry and I would play outside for hours, swinging from the tall bay trees on long hanging wild grapevines. We could swing out over the creek and drop into the water. Larry remembers swinging so high back into a tree that he almost got knocked out. The creek was very shallow during the warm season. I learned to swim in that creek. My dad had been a swimming instructor at UC Berkeley when he was a student, so I was always very proud that he taught me to swim. Two scary things in the water were the crayfish and the underwater rusty car, which I slipped onto once and cut my foot, followed by lots of blood and screaming. Later, we saw a doctor and got a tetanus shot.

My parents worked very hard on that remote place. My dad and Larry would collect rounded river rocks in the wheelbarrow, and they completed a nice rock wall in the outdoor kitchen and dining area. All of the cement, as well as camping and cooking supplies, needed to be carried in across the creek from where we parked. One spring when the creek was high, my dad carried me across on his back. I still can't believe how hard they worked just getting us in and out of there each trip. As time went on, my parents could no longer do all that work, lost interest in the place, and it was sold.

Thereafter, we continued camping and fishing all over Northern California and Oregon. It wasn't until many years later that we stayed in resorts—at Shasta Lake, Bucks Lake, and in Oregon. At Bucks Lake we rented horses for hourly rides. I remember it costing only fifty cents an hour. Today it can be fifty dollars an hour. I grew to love hiking as my main outdoor interest in my teenage years.

In addition to those early camping trips, my aunt Dawn and uncle Dan Rose owned a cabin on the American River along Highway 50 in California. We spent many wonderful summers there with our cousins Greg and Steve. Sometimes, my dad and uncle would return to the Bay Area for work, but the children and moms would stay the week until the dads returned the next weekend. Dawn was my mom's sister, and they were very close. She was delightful, fun, and cheerful, always sparkling, and I loved her. I was her only niece and I think the feeling was mutual.

The children always did a lot of swimming in the river there, floating downstream on inner tubes, jumping into the river from a big rock. We also hiked up to the flume above the cabin, up and down the river, crossed the bridge to go to McCann's resort to buy milk and bread, and we were always fishing and eating fresh trout for breakfast. The cabin was across the river from the highway, and it was a favorite pastime with our cousins to wave and yell across to the passing logging trucks, shouting, "Hey Joe!" to see if we could get them to honk their big horns. They often did. The traffic didn't seem to bother us in those days at all. Sometimes there would be an auto show up at Lake Tahoe and we would see colorful old cars driving east on their way to Echo Summit and down to the lake. My cousin Greg and his large family still enjoy their cabin today, though it had to be completely rebuilt many years ago after it burned to the ground during a forest fire. The bridge that crosses the river to the cluster of cabins has also been replaced because the American River washed it out more than once.

In addition to camping, my family visited San Francisco fairly often for shopping, special dinners, and museums. Chinatown was a favorite spot, searching for fun paper flowers, little statues, and fortune cookies in the small shops. We usually went to a small downstairs restaurant that my parents had frequented when they'd been in college. My mother had worked at the City of Paris department store, and it was a beautiful sight at Christmas time with its huge tree extending up three floors. It was fun to go up in the elevator and look over the balcony at the decorations on all the levels. On Market Street, the top of the Emporium had rides and a Santa Claus, and Union Square was beautifully decorated. In those days, it was easy to drive to San Francisco or take the bus and walk around. Commuter traffic from Marin County, over the Golden Gate Bridge, was not the problem that it is today.

Memorable things we did were seeing a traveling Van Gogh exhibit, a colorful Matisse show displaying his impressive cutouts from his later years, and visiting the Academy of Sciences and the San Francisco Zoo, where I fell in love with "Puddles" the hippopotamus. Another memory is of dressing up in our best clothes to see Margot Fonteyn dance in *Swan Lake* with the Saddler's Wells Ballet. Looking back, I treasure the fact that our parents exposed us to culture and camping—a balance I've enjoyed all my life.

Troubles were surfacing at home when I was ten. The neighborhood was reporting a night prowler, and everyone was worried. I started having sleep problems after my fifth grade teacher, Mr. Costello, read us "The Pit and the Pendulum" by Edgar Allan Poe. I started waking my parents up nightly, and my father walked me all around the house showing me that the doors were locked. Even today, I am impressed by his loving patience. My brother was having other difficulties, and I recall him arguing with my father in his room upstairs. The argument was followed by a shoving fistfight. My mother was trying to break it up, and I was hanging on the stairway pleading for them to stop. My father was also having a lot of trouble at work when one of his partners quit and the firm had to be reorganized. It was a tough time, and I could feel all the tension at home.

My parents had always enjoyed their evening scotch and bourbon together, but now my brother and I began to feel like outsiders to the cocktail hour. Without saying why, we each disappeared into our own rooms until dinnertime. I remember many conversations at the table when my dad had to have the last word, and I was learning that it was hard to project my own ideas with him. My best listener and confidante after school was my mother; we often sat at the kitchen table and talked. If I cried, she would always say it was good to get out the frustrations. We had happy times together, also, when we went shopping for used furniture, clothes, or fabric and when she taught me how to sew.

When I was about twelve, my father developed heart disease and was suddenly having angina pains at home. I felt very worried when I heard him moaning in the bedroom. At that time, he was only about forty-two and under the care of a doctor for years thereafter. His body had an inability to handle cholesterol, and in those days, there wasn't much they could do for patients except give them pain medication and diet guidelines. My mother was diligent about preparing healthy, low-cholesterol meals, but we were worried about him for years thereafter.

Eventually, when he was fifty-nine, he had open-heart surgery in San Francisco at a time when it was a new procedure. He came through it well. He was healthy for the next eleven years but died of pneumonia in October 1984, after his second open-heart surgery when he was seventy. My mother outlived him by twenty years and died of pneumonia in October 2004 when she was ninety-one.

During my early teens, I started making friends with, what my mother called, the "wrong crowd." In sixth grade, I went steady with a boy and went to coed parties where we played kissing games. It was all pretty innocent, with no sex, drinking, or drugs, but my mother finally put her foot down and refused to let me go to a particular party. I was so angry I filled a whole tablet with cursive lines of "I hate my mother!" which she later found in the garbage can. Looking back, I think she was right about that group. Until the day she died, I never told her about climbing out of my bedroom window with a girlfriend in the middle of the night and walking all the way across the freeway and into Mill Valley to look into a boy's window. Then the gal and I walked all the way back, a distance of about eight miles, round trip; we crawled back into bed, and my parents never knew. One time, I tried smoking in the bathroom at home and thought, "Yuck," and never did it again until I tried marijuana in my late twenties. That, too, was a one-time deal. In high school eventually, I became involved with a wonderful group of kids who were more academically and musically inclined.

During my teenage years, we didn't do as many camping trips as a family. My brother Larry became very interested in boats, both motor and sailboats. When I was in high school, our parents bought a twenty-two-foot cabin cruiser that we took up into the Sacramento Delta on overnight trips. I was happy that they named it "The Nancy," but I always felt restless on boats and got very seasick crossing the north bay. Nonetheless, they were interesting trips. One Thanksgiving, we pulled ashore in the Delta and had what my dad would always call "starboard turkey" when he carved the right side of the bird. (To remember the right and left of the boat, we always said, "Johnny LEFT port.") He was very cheerful and clever with humorous remarks.

One of our last camping trips together was to Lakes Basin Recreation Area near Graeagle, California. One of my high school friends, Francie Oman, and her family had a tradition of camping there every summer. They invited us to join them in 1959 when I was sixteen. We hiked up to Long Lake and along the Bear Lake loop. I fell in love with the place that summer and still go there today, over fifty years later. It is a beautiful lake-strewn area at about 6,500 feet, with a backdrop of the Sierra Buttes and Mount Elwell. Summer wildflowers abound. One never tires of the variety of hiking trails that lie below the Pacific Crest Trail in Sierra and Plumas Counties. All the trails are easily accessible without extremely high altitudes as in Yosemite or the Southern Sierra.

Also, when I was sixteen and a sophomore in high school, we moved from Strawberry across the freeway into the wooded West Blithedale Canyon in Mill Valley. We bought a brown shingle house, at 78 Coronet Avenue, with a view of the mountain. Now, we were closer to Mount Tamalpais, high school friends, and within walking distance to the historic downtown. We were on a west-facing slope in a clearing with afternoon sun, but also surrounded by oaks, bays, and redwoods. The house was modest in size with only two bedrooms and one bath, but my parents got busy adding a bathroom and improving a basement room for their bedroom. My father built a big walk-in closet and many storage cupboards. A few years ago, I got to see the inside of the house again, and his woodwork was still there, as were many of the plants he had put into his garden design.

Before a new house was built on the lot next door, I loved sitting on the slope with a beautiful view of Mount Tamalpais. From where I sat, I could see the outline of the "Sleeping Maiden," which is the name the early native people gave the profile along the ridge that resembled a woman at rest. The mountain, at 2,571 feet high, has a remarkable setting where it overlooks the Pacific Ocean to the west and the San Francisco Bay Area to the southeast. From my viewpoint, I could see the wooded slopes and canyons that were often blanketed with cascading evening fog, and I could smell the aroma of bay and redwood trees. This was my favorite spot to sit and contemplate whatever happiness, confusion, or sadness I felt during those teenage years.

In high school, I was busy with my friends and activities. I was very active in drama and the high school choir, in addition to being a good student. I took piano lessons, but I wasn't self-disciplined in my practice. However, Larry and I did get very good on banjo and guitar, often playing together at home or school events. I also played and performed with Nancy Piver who was a talented friend. The timing of our youth coincided with the emergence of folk music with the Weavers, Pete Seeger, the Kingston Trio, and later, Joan Baez, Judy Collins, and Bob Dylan. My junior and senior years, our high school choir did musicals "Paint Your Wagon," "Brigadoon," and "The Pajama Game" in which I had a lead role. The choir also performed at the opening ceremony of the 1960 Winter Olympics in Squaw Valley. Our fabulous and patient choral leader was Robert Greenwood who lived well into his nineties many years after we graduated. When I was in high school, I wanted to take private voice lessons, but I was disappointed when my parents didn't agree, even though I had a very good soprano voice. I had to settle for singing in the shower. Looking back, I don't know why they said no, but I did take voice in college and went on to sing in several choirs.

This, also, was the period of my life when I became interested in hiking and driving to the beaches. On afternoons and weekends, my parents were often willing to loan me our second car, a cute turquoise English Ford that my mother and I had found in a used car lot. I was a good driver, but looking back, I am amazed that they trusted me to drive the steep, winding roads to Stinson Beach. Having a driver's license in Mill Valley was a rite of passage for a teenager, and most of us became very good drivers. I also loved hiking and sketching on Mount Tamalpais trails with friends. I loved the freedom of getting older, and Mill Valley was a unique place in which to grow up; one could step out the door and hike many trails beneath towering redwoods and along bubbling streams heading to the bay. I was lucky to have a group of friends who loved the outdoors, and I even had a boyfriend whose room was like a science lab, including fifty-seven mice in cages. He loved to hike and photograph and went on to raise heirloom seeds in Iowa. Sometimes I would hike with one or two friends and occasionally large groups. One spring, a big group of us went to Tennessee Valley, which was then private ranch land. Innocently, we hiked along a ridgeline and all started rolling big boulders down the grassy slopes into the valley. Soon a rancher appeared on his horse and told us to stop immediately. He had cattle and calves below. Understandably, he asked us to get off his property. Today, that property is part of the Golden Gate National Recreation Area and heavily used by hikers, cyclists, and horseback riders. I've been back many times, but have never forgotten my first visit there and the lesson well learned.

Muir Woods National Monument was over the hill from Mill Valley and was another place we often hiked amid the towering coastal redwoods and pungent California bay trees. People from all over the world came to visit the monument, but we could go whenever we wanted. Also, within an hour's drive were several coastal beaches: Muir Beach, Stinson Beach, and Point Reyes. At a young age, I realized I was growing up in a very special area with easy access to pristine outdoor places. Though I may have taken them for granted then, these experiences would become a theme throughout my life.

Mill Valley in the 1950s and '60s was a very special place to live during my adolescence and high school years. The downtown was unpretentious and very scenic with the backdrop of Mount Tamalpais, the old railroad/ bus depot, and there were the remains of an old lumber mill in Old Mill Park. The walk from our house to town went through a neighborhood of old houses, a redwood grove, over a creek and past the Bardea's Shoe Repair. The Mill Valley Market was next to the City Hall, and there was a Chinese grocery, the Sequoia Theater, a Ben Franklin Five-and-Dime, Varney's Hardware, two pet stores, Bell's Kiddie Shop, Mosher's Shoes, the Men's Shop, the R & M shop, Strawbridge's Stationery, Dimitroff's

Art and Frame shop, and two bakeries, as well as the Redwood Bookstore and Mayer's Department Store. The Mosher, Dimitroff, and Varney kids all went to school with us, as well as many others whose parents worked in town. It was a different town back then, as it is now replaced by galleries, coffee chains, and expensive clothing stores. The Mill Valley Market survives, as do the theater and the Depot, which is now a café and bookstore. And, the redwoods still stand as sentries to the downtown plaza.

When Larry was a senior in high school, he continued his interest in boats. He was designing trimarans, and he and our father built one of his boats in our front driveway. When he graduated from high school, he went to college at the University of Oregon for about a year. Eventually, he decided that college wasn't for him, and after returning home, he continued being very involved in boat designing. My parents helped him get started with a home office. Even at a young age, he showed a skill and talent for designing trimarans and other boats. In later years, he would sell many of his plans for Williams trimarans, which can still be seen on San Francisco Bay and in Seattle. He also built his own forty-two-foot ferro-cement boat in Sausalito and lived on it for many years. He named it the "Clarence A. Marcy" after our grandfather. It was a square-rigged sailboat. In addition to designing, Larry sailed on other large boats to the South Seas as a deckhand. For many years, he lived on the Sausalito waterfront, earning a modest living by designing and doing heavy marine engine repair.

Larry and I both attended Tamalpais High School, which was unique with its Spanish architecture and location overlooking Richardson Bay. Students had attended since 1908, and we had friends whose parents had attended. Larry graduated in 1959, and I followed in 1961. I enjoyed high school and had many friends and activities. I was editor of the Tamalpais News in my senior year. My friends were smart and fun, and we had many outings and activities outside of school. Academically, I was an honor student, but my weaknesses were in math and chemistry. My chemistry teacher, Mr. Reneau, said I was "certainly an A+ as a person" when I nearly failed an exam. My strengths were English, Spanish, history, and art, in addition to music.

After I graduated, I enrolled at UC Santa Barbara and lived in a dorm, but only stayed one semester. I didn't connect with friends I enjoyed and did poorly in math and science but was too hesitant to ask for help. My algebra teacher said, "Where have you been all semester? Why didn't you come earlier for help?" and I barely passed with a C. Biology was even worse. I spent many hours studying, but my mind wandered over pages about DNA and other complicated things. I didn't even know what to ask. Going to college was a shock, and I was very homesick for my family and friends who had scattered to various colleges. As a result, I ended up returning to Mill Valley after the holidays and enrolling at Marin Community College in Kentfield, where I again had a view of my favorite mountain.

There, I found my feet again and made many new friends, especially in the art and music departments. Those departments at Marin had excellent teachers. I took art classes, including printmaking, where I learned etching, silk screen, lithography, and woodblock printing. I enjoyed art history where I gathered with newfound friends for study groups to learn the styles of many famous artists. All of the students were about my age, but we befriended a sixty-five year-old art student, a widow who had survived cancer, and was a fun spirit for us all. Sometimes we would study at her view home in Sausalito where we could overlook San Francisco Bay.

My time at College of Marin coincided with the presidency of John F. Kennedy who had been elected in November 1960. His short presidency had started in January 1961, when I was a senior in high school, and continued when I enrolled at College of Marin. In October 1962, the Cuban Missile Crisis gripped our country with fear, though it seemed short lived at the time. Then on November 22, 1963, when I was paying for lunch at the school cafeteria, I was informed by the cashier behind the counter that President Kennedy had just been assassinated in Texas. That moment is frozen in time. I knew my mother was on campus that day, so I went directly to her art studio and was the first to tell her. We agreed to go home together to Mill Valley and remained glued to the black-and-white television for several days as we watched the swearing in of Lyndon Johnson, the subsequent murder of the assassin J. Harvey Oswald, and the memorable funeral in Washington, DC. The whole country stood still. Nothing like it had occurred in recent history.

My best friend at College of Marin was Loren Partridge, a fellow art student. Loren had also grown up in Mill Valley, but I hadn't known her because she'd gone to high school in Oak Creek Canyon near Sedona, Arizona. Our parents had known each other through the design community in Marin and San Francisco. Loren and I rented an apartment together in Kentfield while attending College of Marin and developed friendships there with other art students. Loren was the granddaughter of Imogen Cunningham, the well-known San Francisco photographer, and the etcher Roi Partridge.

One time Loren and I visited Imogen at her home in San Francisco on Green Street. Imogen sat me on her back porch and took a portrait of me with a camera she was testing for Polaroid. A few years later, she gave me the print as a gift. Oh, how I wish she had signed it, but it only has her exposure scribblings on the back. It is framed on my wall. Another time, we picked up Imogen and went to Chinatown, where we had dinner with her good friend Ruth Osawa, the San Francisco sculptor. I also wish I had a picture of that night or had kept a diary.

I do remember well, however, that Imogen would throw on her black cape with the peace symbol pin always in place every time we went out with her. She was spry and feisty and must have been nearing her eighties when I knew her.

After College of Marin, Loren and I both enrolled at San Francisco State University. We rented a flat with two other gals in San Francisco on Third Avenue near Golden Gate Park. From there, we could walk a couple of blocks to catch the N Judah metro rail to the university or downtown. It turned out, however, that neither of us liked living in San Francisco because attempts were made, more than once, to break into our apartment while we were inside. We could see the flashlight scanning the hinges and locks and shouted to scare the culprits away.

We felt unsafe, so we moved back to Marin where we rented an apartment in Sausalito up on the hill. We enjoyed being able to walk downtown to the bookstore and the waterfront and wished we were old enough to go to the No Name Bar with friends. We also enjoyed meeting friends in the plaza and made a movie with Steve Hopper and Jon Sanford, whom we had known at College of Marin. They were more offbeat than we, but we enjoyed the fun and didn't drop out of school like many others did.

One time the four of us drove in Jon's four-wheel drive Toyota all over hills in the Marin Headlands at night and another time even up the steps at the local elementary school. It was thrilling to be disobedient, and luckily we were never caught. Also, in those days, there was a notorious woman, Juanita, who ran a restaurant in Sausalito. She was brash, loud, impolite, legendary in her large tent dresses, and known all over Marin County. We often went there to watch the show and sample the lifestyle of the hippies and waterfront locals.

During the summers, when I was nineteen and twenty, I was fortunate to work at Madrona Inn on Orcas Island in the San Juan Islands of Washington. The inn was owned by the family of my high school friend Francie Oman who accompanied me there for two summers. I loved my job as a cottage girl, cleaning rustic cabins on a wooded, scenic peninsula. Each cabin was nestled in the red-bark Madrone trees and overlooked the bay. If I and my coworker, Sheila, worked rapidly enough, we had the rest of the day off, unlike the waitresses who worked three meals a day. We used the time to hike to and from the quaint town of Eastsound or nap in our rooms under piles of quilts on foggy afternoons. We stayed up late most nights singing by driftwood campfires on the beaches, where I led the folk singing with my guitar. We were eleven girls working and living alone in a big, old Victorian house on the property, and we were all innocently tasting freedom those summers. Returning home to college at the end of the summers was always a tough adjustment for us all.

About a year later, in 1964, I met up again with Wes Hildreth in Mill Valley. He and I had dated briefly when I was about sixteen, but now I was twenty-one and more independent. He was twenty-six, had graduated from Harvard and traveled the world, and was home for the summer. We discovered a common interest in outdoor adventure and hiking. On a trip in northern California, we climbed Mount Lassen—an easy ascent, but our first together. A bond was developed. Then Wes left on a prearranged trip to Sweden and more European travel, but he stayed in touch with letters. I went back to San Francisco State, but didn't complete the semester because Wes and I decided to get married in London. My parents agreed easily, bought me a ticket, gave me a nice engagement party, and helped me prepare for the trip. My mom and I enjoyed shopping trips when she bought me a beautiful warm coat and clothing for a London winter. I shipped a trunk to London and flew out of San Francisco on Christmas Eve 1964.

Orlando B. Marcy, about 1900, great-grandfather

Irena R. Marcy, about 1890, great-grandmother

Irena R. Marcy with her sons, Howard and Clarence (right), about 1894

Nellie Fine Marcy (standing) about 1910

Effie Sherrer Williams, about 1900 (my father's mother who died in 1918 when he was four)

Albert Williams (grandfather) with Albie (left) and
my father Edward (right) about 1918

Ferne Marcy Williams, 1916 (photo by Clarence Marcy)

Edward and Ferne Wiliams, honeymoon 1937 Big Bear Lake, California

Nancy and Larry Williams, 1944, Redwood City, California

Nancy, age five

Nancy Williams and Muffy, November 1964

CHAPTER 2

The Non-Muir Trail

Wes used to say he didn't want to hike the John Muir Trail. That would be too easy, and anyone could do it. He called it a freeway. So he and I chose the term "the Non-Muir Trail," and, in a sense, that's what we did as a lifestyle together from 1965 to 1972. Our "trail" became a way of life filled with travel and adventure, many knapsack routes in the back country of California and beyond, but anchored by school and temporary jobs as we prepared for a future together.

I was twenty-one when Wes Hildreth and I married on New Year's Eve 1964/65 in London, England. Wes made all the arrangements, before I arrived, for a small church wedding at Saint John-at-Hampstead. Neither of us were religious, and I had never been baptized, but Wes convinced the pastor to perform the simple ceremony at this Church of England. It was a small stone church adorned by ivy, and the evening wedding by candlelight was very intimate and special. George Cagwin, a Mill Valley friend of ours, was the best man and had come from Germany where he was with the National Guard. We stifled giggles throughout the ceremony, even though we had met with the pastor a few days before discussing our serious commitment. Michael Isador, an American pianist residing in London, played the organ. Wes had befriended him and had been staying at his London flat, almost under the grand piano in the living room. Michael played a processional used for the queen, plus "Simple Gifts" by Aaron Copland. To this day, I always take a meaningful pause when I hear those pieces.

Before the ceremony, I had flown to London lugging a guitar, a huge suitcase, and carry-on bags I could hardly manage. They didn't have rules for carry-ons in those days, just whatever you could manage was allowed. I even took a set of stainless flatware that was a wedding present from family friends. Seems so silly now, but we used it in our tiny apartment and eventually shipped it all back in a trunk. I still use that flatware more than fifty years later. Customs hesitated when I gave them less information than they wanted about my arrival. Wes had said to tell them I was just visiting the country, but apparently one look at this young gal with a full set of flatware made them wonder. The agent asked who was meeting me, I gave Wes's name, and he interviewed him in the lobby and came back to say in his saucy British accent, "Why didn't you tell me you were getting married? Congratulations!" *Stamp!* Previous to that, as I deplaned, lugging my stuff down the stairs from the BOAC jet onto the tarmac, I had seen Wes up on the outdoor deck waiting area, waving *big* arms to greet me. These days, no one could get through security to do that.

Wes and I stayed at Michael Isador's flat for a few days until the wedding. I was introduced to matzo, British tea, and not much else in the bachelors' kitchen. Michael's roommate was away, so he had space to accommodate us for a few days. After the wedding, we were to move into the flat Wes had rented for us. While we were at Michael's, we were treated to him practicing on his grand piano. He had been a child prodigy when growing up in Pennsylvania, had debuted as a soloist at a young age in the United States, and now in his twenties, he was to perform Tchaikovsky's Piano Concerto #1 at the Royal Albert Hall a few weeks later; naturally, we saw him from balcony seats when that occurred. Imagine sleeping with that fabulous music in the next room! But I was so jet-lagged, I could have slept through anything, and I did.

The day of the wedding I was alone, bathing and dressing. I remember a big, old bathtub with hot water from the Ascot water heater alongside. I was both happy and sad. It seemed bittersweet, and the thought crossed my mind that it should be nicer than this getting ready for my wedding; even though I was very much in love, I missed my family and close friends. I dressed alone, putting on the olive-green velveteen dress I had made myself. It had a princess-style high waist and fit perfectly. Black shoes and a crown of dried flowers on my head, I had never dreamed of a traditional white dress and wedding. But I did want a fresh bouquet, and I asked Wes and George to buy me one. They came back with a colorful nosegay of freesias. The aroma was wonderful in the London winter. They did well to find them and were proud.

We took a London taxi to the church. That was a new experience for me, as was everything else for a gal who had never been abroad before. The wedding party consisted of Wes and me, George as best man, and Michael on the organ. The guests were a half a dozen people I had never met but who were friends of Michael's and Wes's. They were a small mix of young Brits and Americans living abroad. The small ornate church was quaint and chilly, but after the ceremony, Wes and I signed the fancy marriage certificate, and we all went to a nice, cozy restaurant that Wes had arranged for our small party. Outside, George surprised us all by setting off firecrackers!

That night, we went straight to our rented flat at 11 Ellsworthy Terrace. It was three flights up on the top floor with one gable window and just on the edge of Primrose Hill and Regents Park. Our landladies, Madge and Mum, had surprised us with flowers in the room and the bedding turned back. They had even put schillings in the heater to warm the place up. We didn't see them that night, but they were, thereafter, good entertainment for us. The twin beds were pushed together, and the bed was made for us. I had not wanted a white wedding dress, but someone from home had gifted me a gorgeous white nightgown, which was a big surprise.

The next day, we rented a Morris Mini and started out on the left side of the road for our winter honeymoon in Cornwall. That Morris fit between every hedgerow lane we traveled. First, we visited Stonehenge, which was not surrounded by cyclone fencing as it is today. We were able to walk right up to the stones, looking at them from every angle. It was cold but beautiful out on the plain. Then we went on to Salisbury Cathedral. Of course, I had never seen such a place—huge, beautiful, and very cold inside where our voices echoed. For several days, we traveled in Cornwall, visiting coastal towns and staying each night in a B&B, some very cute and all found on the spur of the moment because we were off season and the weather was dreary. In Mousehole, we took a photo in front of the Keigwin Arms pub in honor of our friend George Cagwin.

Back in London, we needed to find jobs to support this adventure and pay the rent. We only planned to stay a few months but never revealed that in the interviews. I wept on street corners, feeling inexperienced and terrified of the interviews, but managed to land myself a typing job at the Royal Institute of British Architects (RIBA). I had a good letter of recommendation from my dad's landscape architecture firm in San Francisco where I had worked occasionally and had good training under the head secretary. She raved about me on paper, and it did the trick. I ended up in the typing pool with some cockney gals, but was quickly moved into an office that assisted students looking for architecture colleges in England. My office group consisted of Christine, who had "rescued" me from the typing pool, and three guys, all equally hilarious. We laughed hard each day; they loved imitating my American accent, and I their varied British tongues. They had never heard the word "alphabetize" and always told me "to put in alphabetical order." The maids brought coffee each morning and tea and biscuits each afternoon. Lunch could be purchased upstairs in a cafeteria, but I often took off to a museum for a quick viewing. One time Wes showed up and startled me in a museum because I had been telling him I couldn't look at any men in the museums because they would sidle up to me and try to pick me up.

Wes got a job teaching at a boys' school, but that lasted only a few days because they were so rude and naughty. With no teaching experience, why would anyone want to teach naughty British schoolboys? He ended up, instead, with a job doing quiet research at London School of Economics. We weren't exactly raking in the dough, but we were saving enough to buy tickets home on the *Queen Mary*, and money to travel to France, Spain, and Switzerland that next spring.

In London, back at the flat, our landladies Madge and Mum were right out of a Charles Dickens novel. Mum was tall and quiet, Madge short and fat. We never saw them that winter without their huge tweed overcoats, well worn and torn in places. I don't think they ever heated their basement flat, and it was a hovel. We never knew their story, but we'll never forget them. If we were a day late on the rent because we hadn't been paid, Mum would wait silently on the landing. I would smile and walk right by, but we always paid. Most memorable was the time she waited on the landing to say, "Winnie's dead." Winston Churchill had passed away on January 24, 1965, at the age of ninety, and all of London was at a standstill. We stayed up all night in line over Westminster Bridge to see him lying in state, closed casket at Westminster Hall. The next day, sunny but cold, we stood on steps along with hundreds of others watching the funeral procession through Trafalgar Square.

We were very busy that winter with our jobs and activities. I walked to and from my job, all the way across Regents Park, in high heels each day because I preferred it to the men teasing and pinching me on the crowded underground trains. Young women were targets in a way that would be considered harassment these days. I learned how to go to the shops for hamburger called minced meat, pasta, and winter vegetables. We ate a lot of spaghetti that winter because both my repertoire and our budget were small. Our kitchen was tiny with a small stove, table, refrigerator, and skylight all under a sloped ceiling. The bathroom was just that, with only a tub, and the shared loo was just at the landing below. The friendly young, male Indian student who lived the next floor down often invited me for late afternoon tea with evaporated milk and a lump of sugar. I recall fun, friendly conversations and how unique it was to have a male friend. It was very easy to meet people our age in London back then. Americans were respected, and we were invited to friends' homes. Once I met a gal on a street corner who assisted me as I struggled with dust in a contact lens; before I knew it, she had invited us to dinner a few days later.

Wes was a long-distance runner, so he did exercises each morning or evening in our flat before his runs. It was a new experience for me to see such dedication to an exercise routine. I sometimes did sit-ups and stretches as well. I often drew him baths to return to after long runs. On weekends, we would take public transportation everywhere and often to areas where he could participate in long-distance races. I always bundled up to wait for him at the site, sometimes holding the stopwatch for recording times and visiting with others while I waited. I didn't consider running myself at that time, but that came later in our marriage. For now, I walked all over London for my exercise.

London was rich with experiences for us. With my art history background, I loved visiting the museums, especially the Tate with its Turner paintings, and the British Museum. I recall the ominous ravens at the Tower of London near the chopping block where Anne Boleyn and many others had lost their heads. I loved a performance of Saint Matthew's Passion at Saint Paul's Cathedral because I had previously performed it at home with my community chorus. A choir with British schoolboy sopranos was pure, beautiful music. In another performance, we saw Handel's Messiah, with a cathedral sound not to be matched. In addition, tickets to major shows were cheap, and we often saw live performances, plays, or musicals. The musical *Oliver* was a real treat to see in London where it had been running since in the early 1960s.

Early during our stay in London, we visited Notting Hill and Portobello Road with all its unique shops and colorful people milling about, some selling wares or roasting chestnuts on open fires. It was crowded on a weekend, and we had been told to watch out for pickpockets. Sure enough, after that day, I noticed I had lost the treasured wristwatch that had been given to me by my parents as a high school graduation present. It had probably fallen off and not been stolen but found by some lucky soul. We replaced it at a jewelry store, but I was sad to lose the original.

We ventured outside London a few times, once to visit my friend Christine's family in Oxford. She toured us around on foot, and we enjoyed a nice meal with her parents at their home. Everywhere that winter it was cold, so we appreciated sunny days; that's how I recall Oxford that day. In London and Oxford, flowers were noticeable in parks and at vendors' stands. The British knew how to cheer up in dreary weather; I loved the freesias, daffodils, and primroses as they appeared. Kew Gardens was, of course, amazing, as were the gardens at Hampton Court.

When the time came for us to leave London to travel to France and Spain in the spring of 1965, we were somewhat reluctant to leave, but also eager to travel. I had turned twenty-two and was given a fun send-off by my working friends at the RIBA. Before we left London, Wes tucked my dried wedding bouquet into a burrow, high up in an old oak tree on Primrose Hill, as I watched from below. Madge and Mum, nearby, couldn't imagine what we were doing. The only person we ever saw again, aside from George, was Michael Isador, who eventually came to live in Mill

Valley. By that time, he had decided to take a break from the stresses of performing. He eventually married, lived in Europe, and was sought after as a talented accompanist. Later, he became director of the arts program at Bryn Mawr College in Pennsylvania.

Wes and I traveled by train overland to Dover where we loaded onto a boat to cross the English Channel by night en route to Calais. I played folk songs on my guitar in the dim light on the train that took us all the way into Paris where we had arranged to meet our friend George. He came from his National Guard duties in Germany to meet us with his Volkswagen and new British girlfriend, Julia, who would take a brief break from her job in Geneva, Switzerland. After a week or so, Julia would return to work, and Wes, George, and I would travel in his car south to Spain. In Paris, we saw many famous sites, but also stood on street corners, trying to make decisions about what to do and where to eat. Understandably, Wes was tired of being the guide, but none of the rest of us knew French or where to go. As frustrating as this was, we did manage to visit museums and major sites. Again, I enjoyed the art museums and a chance to see many of the paintings I had only seen in books. We did a whirlwind tour, up and down out of metro stations. Musicians in the underground stations were remarkably entertaining where the acoustics helped the music resound. Most impressive was the architecture of famous buildings, cathedrals, and the Seine and Luxembourg Gardens. Wes had traveled the world alone on a Sheldon Traveling Fellowship after graduating from Harvard, but I was a wide-eyed gal who had never been abroad.

After leaving France, we crossed the Pyrenees Range and traveled up to Guernica, which was familiar to me because of the Picasso mural (1937) of the same name. The painting had been done to bring attention to the horror of the bombings of the Basque community by the Nazis during the Spanish Civil War. Indeed, in 1965, we could still feel the tensions as we observed Guardia Civil on corners. People were hushed and reluctant to speak out even then. Franco was still in power in Spain. Though our spirits were dampened by this, we still had fun joining in at a Basque festival held high above the town, reached by a long hike up a hill. It was colorful and fun with music and good food.

After leaving Guernica we headed south in George's little Volkswagen. We had no itinerary, just a plan to travel down the center of the country seeing the landscape, major towns, and cities. We stayed in cheap hotels and hostels wherever we ended up each night. Some were very rustic, and in one, we slept on a mattress filled with hay, though covered by clean sheets. I recall the beautiful dry landscape with olive groves and rolling hills. We all still laugh today about the donkey who brayed loudly and let "everything" hang down when we stopped thc car. In the countryside, we occasionally talked with farmers, all still reluctant to speak about the political situation, but Wes could speak enough Spanish to engage in some conversation, and George and I could understand a bit but were shy about speaking. I recall one hostel where we sat with peasant workers in a poorly lit room while Wes engaged them in a discussion of their political views.

Spain had the aroma of olive oil in every town and city, no matter how small. I was overdosed on the smell then, though I had loved it before and still do today. We drank a lot of orange soda instead of water and ate whatever we could afford. Bread and cheese were staples on the road each day. We were on a slim budget, but you could travel through Europe on five dollars a day back then just as the guidebook said.

The fanciest meal I recall was at a restaurant in Madrid where we experienced paella for the first time. I recall the guys making comments about the richness of the food as we examined what we were eating. Also, in Madrid I visited the Museo del Prado where I remember standing in front of famous paintings by Hieronymus Bosch (*The Garden of Early Delights*) and Diego Velazquez (*Las Meninas*) that I had seen in my college texts. As we traveled south, we passed through towns and cities and visited many cathedrals, sometimes joking, "Un otro cateedral" (another cathedral)! To this day, I can picture the famous cathedral high on the hill in Toledo that I recognized from a landscape painting by El Greco, who lived in Toledo for several decades.

We headed south to Granada, saw elevated aqueducts, and stood in front of the Alhambra. I knew I should see the museums, but we didn't. I reluctantly went along with the guys who wanted to continue south, a lasting regret. After Granada, we ended up in Malaga, where we attended a gory bullfight, really an awful spectacle as I didn't share Hemingway's fascination other than knowing it was part of experiencing Spain. Next, we went across to Gibraltar, which was still a British territory, and I felt comfortable hearing English spoken again as we passed curio shops and tearooms. We saw the Rock of Gibraltar and the famous monkeys. I can still remember looking south to Algiers in the distance, impressed with how close it was.

Back on the southern coastline, we headed east and eventually ended up at a beach outside Barcelona. There, we used very poor judgment and left everything in the car while we took a swim in the Mediterranean. I was dressed only in a swimming suit under my dress and wore my prescription sunglasses. The guys had on shorts for running and swimming. When we returned to the car, it had been robbed, and almost everything was gone—suitcases, my purse, camera, glasses, contact lenses, all money, travelers' checks, boat tickets for the Queen Mary and passports. Luckily, George still had his car keys, and they did not take my guitar, which I still have today. We had been innocent and dumb. As a result, we headed straight for the American consulate to get new passports and ask for a loan. They issued us passports, but would not loan us money. We were really angry, but luckily, George had a little money still. I hardly remember seeing Barcelona, except the Gaudi (another cathedral), because we soon departed for a long overnight drive to Geneva, Switzerland, where George had relatives. Somehow, even without car papers, we managed to get through customs at the border.

We had left a forwarding address with the consulate, and about a week later our cancelled passports, boat tickets, and travelers' checks, but not the camera, were returned to George's Swiss relatives by mail. Apparently, they had been dropped into a mailbox addressed to the consulate headquarters in Barcelona. Those were sophisticated thieves, even somewhat thoughtful. Amazingly, we were told, that happened in those days. Meanwhile, Wes had called his uncle Jim in Connecticut, who had wired him some money to get home. We shopped for some replacement clothes, basics such as underwear so I could get out of my swimming suit. (I had to wear my prescription sunglasses day and night all the way home to California several weeks later.) While we waited and visited in Geneva, we saw Julia where she worked near Lake Geneva. We took a beautiful drive around the lake and up to the picturesque village of Grindelvald. There we hiked high up on the slopes seeing chalets, a village festival, and beautiful, healthy Swiss cows.

Soon we said goodbye to George and Julia, who by this time were planning their wedding in her home country of England. We traveled back to France and on to Normandy, sometimes by public transport and eventually by hitchhiking in Normandy. I remember being picked up by a farmer way out in the country. In Bayeux, we didn't take the time to see the famous Bayeux Tapestry, which shows the events before the Norman conquest of England in 1066 at the Battle of Hastings. I can't recall how we finally made it to the American Cemetery near Omaha Beach, but it was a beautiful, sunny day and a very moving sight.

Finally, we worked our way to Cherbourg where we caught the *Queen Mary* home. That was nearly its last year as a passenger ship because more people were flying by then and the Cunard Lines were losing money. Five seasick days would describe that trip for me, but I do remember the fancy dining rooms, the silver and china place settings, and ornate furnishings, as well as the buckets lining the halls. I would eat and throw up, but I was not the only one sick. We sat for each meal at a different table and met many new people. We had a tiny room with bunk beds and a sink the size of a quarter, way down below. We couldn't afford anything better, and it would have been a waste of money since I was so sick. The weather was stormy all the way to New York where I was very happy to see the Statue of Liberty come into view so I could get my feet on land again. Despite my sickness, I have always been glad I had the experience of an ocean voyage across the Atlantic, giving me a sense of the distance between the continents and the harshness of stormy seas.

We were picked up at dockside by Wes's dear uncle Jim, who took us home to Wilton, Connecticut, where I met Aunt Clyde and stayed in their sweet, yellow guest room. Uncle Jim's bedroom upstairs was all decorated with George Washington motif, and Clyde's feminine room was across the hall. She liked to read and stay in bed later in the morning, but she always set Uncle Jim's place at the breakfast table the night before so he could rise early, walk down the hill to the station, and catch the train to work in downtown New York. We traveled with him a couple of times to go sightseeing on our own. We stayed a week before picking up George's car, which had been shipped to New York because he was flying home. Then we took off on a cross-country trip to return home to Mill Valley, arriving in the early summer. It felt free to be traveling back in the wide-open spaces of America again.

Back in Mill Valley that summer of 1965, we rented a small cottage from family friends, and Wes got a summer job with Tom Cagwin's landscaping company, Cagwin and Dorward, planting trees in Novato on a center strip, and I worked for his uncle Charlie Lindsay in his downtown San Francisco office. Charlie and his buddy slipped out each lunchtime for a martini with their meal. He asked me to collect as many parking garage receipts as I could get from the ground or the garbage bins in the garage, so he could write them off on his taxes. He was a character, but we all loved Uncle Charles.

In September, we returned east to Cambridge, where Wes started graduate school in political science at Harvard. We rented a cozy apartment near campus, and I set up an easel and my sewing machine and arranged my cookbooks. I had plans for how I would spend my spare time while Wes studied. Then, I got a full-time job at the Design Research store as the scheduler for furniture deliveries. That was particularly funny since I didn't know the area and had to rely on a map on the wall to make my plans for the drivers each day. Design Research had imports from Scandinavian countries and stores in other American cities as well. My officemate, Tove, was from Norway, and we became good friends. I also became friends with the elderly talented upholsterer who gave me fabric samples from which I made a big, heavy quilt, one side with warm colors, the other with cool. At night, I navigated public transportation and attended Boston Museum School to learn ceramics, sang in a choir, and took French.

After a few months, and coinciding with our first wedding anniversary in December 1965, Wes struggled through a difficult decision to quit grad school. The freedom of those traveling years was probably a big part of that decision. Plus, it was the 1960s, with much unrest among young people in the country due to the Vietnam War and other social changes. We remained in Cambridge working a few more months saving some money. Then we bought a used Volkswagen bus in Boston and traveled back to California, camping in national parks all the way. We named the German vehicle Schussnigg after the Austrian who had opposed Hitler. It was so loaded with our belongings covered by a mattress there was not much headroom for sleeping. Somewhere traveling through the South, I got my long waist-length hair cut short. In Biloxi, Mississippi, we visited the fancy southern home of one of Wes's friends from Harvard. Earlier that morning in a roadside café, we had devoured the best pancakes I remember ever eating—fluffy and light, made from Bisquick. Pancakes were an affordable breakfast. We visited many notable national parks and monuments, but eventually camped at Furnace Creek in Death Valley in the sweltering spring heat, and I asked, "How could anyone live here?"

In the summer and fall of 1966, I resumed my studies of art and music history at San Francisco State, traveling back and forth across the Golden Gate Bridge from Mill Valley. Wes had landed himself a nice seasonal job as a naturalist with the National Park Service in Muir Woods National Monument right over the hill from where we lived. For a hundred dollars a month, we rented a small cottage owned by my parents' friends, Syd and Margaret Williams (no relation to my family). The cottage, on Oakdale Avenue in Mill Valley, had a railroad car design from front to back—living room, bedroom, bath, and kitchen all lined up, but it was cozy and cute. Much to Wes's surprise, I brought home a kitten we named Euridicye, and I discovered that Wes was a tease, trying to hang her by her legs. Needless to say, Euridicye became a very wary, unfriendly cat, but somehow she remained loyal for the few months we owned her and, thereafter, with Wes's sister who adopted her from us.

That first summer back in Mill Valley, we enjoyed family barbecues with Wes's mom, Freddie; brother, Bruce; and sister, Debbie, as well as Debbie's new husband Scott Mills. We had fun gatherings with friends who stopped by, usually at the Mills's—George Cagwin and his new wife, Julia; Larry Jager; Ralph Brott. The group became a hub of activity with fun dinners or picnics at Stinson Beach. Mill Valley in the summer of 1966 was beautiful and still charming in a friendly way. That summer also, Michael Isador (our American pianist friend from London) moved to Mill Valley and joined us socially. He rented a home on Summit Avenue down the street from Freddie where you could hear his piano across the canyon. He had decided to give up concert performing and was looking ahead to a different life with his music. I am sure he didn't expect to encounter banana slugs on his window sill in the deep, moist redwoods surrounding his house. Wes's mother got a panicky call one day about that.

At Muir Woods, Wes ambled up and down the floor of the redwood groves, meeting with the public and giving nature walks. Always learning and photographing with color slide film, he rapidly became an excellent naturalist. He quickly made friends with Jim Morley, who was a part-time photographer who had been coming to Muir Woods for many years. Jim was working on a book about the monument. Sometimes I would meet Jim there and wander with him while he photographed, and he would give me tips for my own photography. By this time my father had given me a Mamiya twin-lens reflex, medium-format camera so I could try black-and-white photography. It was a camera he had purchased in Japan for himself, but was no longer using. One time Jim asked me to hold a branch out of the way while he took a shot of a tall tree. Later when he published a book on Muir Woods, he inscribed a note to me in the front, "For Nancy who held the branch." Jim remained a friend for many years.

That summer of 1966 we also spent some nice weekends in Bolinas where we were loaned a cabin that Katie Mills rented for several years. She told us where the key was hidden, and we were welcome to go whenever we wanted. We usually had the place to ourselves. It was a rustic beach cabin with colorful dishes, and a good collection of Katie's driftwood and seashells, as well as colorful geraniums in boxes outside. Nothing fancy, just small, cozy, and perfect.

Wes enjoyed his long-distance runs from Mill Valley, seven miles over the shoulder of Mount Tamalpais to Stinson Beach, on the Dipsea Trail. He also did loops on the Bolinas Mesa. I often drove the VW to drop him off and pick him up at various points. I used to say I liked driving alone over to the beach so I could listen to rock 'n' roll music blasting on the radio. One time, I misunderstood the directions for the pickup point along the Bolinas Lagoon, and Wes was understandably mad because he had to run a few extra miles to find me. His mother, Freddie, was in the car with me, and I was so upset at being criticized I shouted, "You can have him back!" That remained a family joke for many years.

Many people visited Muir Woods, but no one as famous that season as Chief Justice William O. Douglas and his young wife. Wes alerted me that he would be giving them a private tour through the woods one morning, and I drove myself over the hill to hang out on the forest floor that day with my camera. I shyly stepped out to take a couple of pictures—sadly, underexposed, but recognizable still today. They were very patient, and had it not been for my shyness and feelings of invading their privacy, I might have taken a better photograph. That winter Wes and another ranger, Don Reeser, floated Redwood Creek from Muir Woods all the way down to Muir Beach when the creek was high enough for a small rubber raft. In those days also, there was always a good run of salmon coming up the creek in the winter and spring. We would often see them spawning as far up as Muir Woods. Still today, I can recall the smell of the bay trees among the redwoods. One kid on a school field trip wrote, "My favorite tree is the California bay tree." I always found that amusing in a monument dedicated to the magnificent coastal redwood.

During the summers, we became seasoned hikers in Yosemite National Park. We were fit and full of energy. Our first summer in the Sierra, we drove our VW bus from Marin County every Friday night, got in late, camped, and took off on the trail the next morning, covering a lot of miles that summer. In those days you could hook a Sierra Club cup over your belt and drink water out of every stream without a fear of giardia.

One of our earliest hikes was a climb up Half Dome in flat-soled running shoes. In those days, we didn't need a permit; we set off early from the campground on the valley floor and hiked the ten miles to the base of the cables, pulled ourselves up the granite face, and were on the top for lunch. There was one other person on top that day. Today there would be a line of climbers, bumper to bumper, each required to have a permit from a lottery, weeks ahead. Coming back down the face, hanging onto the cables was terrifying for me; I had to follow Wes closely, whimpering the whole way, but he praised me nonetheless. We hiked up and back twenty miles that day and limped back to the VW at dusk. I can still recall my sore muscles.

Later that summer, I got my first hiking boots, and we climbed Mount Hoffman above May Lake. That was really our first Sierra climb on a traveled route. It was a long hike to a summit that marks the center of Yosemite National Park and has a spectacular view. Pictures show me pointing to the Hoffman Thumb, well above timberline. We were not alone on that summit, but still not too many people.

Another early hike was in Sequoia/Kings Canyon National Park. After camping overnight near Cedar Grove, we started up the trail toward

Junction Meadows, with no particular plan for how far we would go. The colorful wildflowers by the trail were so beautiful along Bubb's Creek that we just kept going until we intersected the John Muir Trail fifteen miles later at Junction Meadows. It runs over two hundred miles from Yosemite to Mount Whitney and is a historical trail that was envisioned as early as 1884 and completed in sections by 1938. The trail parallels the spine of the Sierra Nevada crossing many high passes, the highest being Forester Pass at 13,153 feet. But this was a day hike, so we turned around and descended along the creek trail again, arriving after dark, sore and tired after a thirty-mile day. We tumbled into the VW bus for a well-earned sleep.

By this time, we were hooked and decided to try backpacking so we could camp out in the backcountry. Initially, we got one large backpack for Wes from a tiny, new mountaineering store in San Francisco—Gerry Mountain Sports on Union Square. That store and Smiley's were the only outdoor stores other than army surplus shops at that time. The Ski Hut in Berkeley started up about then too. We were at the beginning of an expanding interest in the backcountry. Within a few years, Sierra Designs, Marmot Mountain, North Face, Royal Robbins, and finally, REI from Seattle were all over the Bay Area and beyond. Hiking and the outdoor sports industry exploded.

With the new Kelty aluminum frame pack, our first overnight trip was in Yosemite from Tuolumne Meadows to Glen Aulin and down the trail past Waterwheel Falls. With the water tumbling over granite, it was beautiful but not much fun. Wes complained bitterly that he was a long-distance runner and felt burdened. He wanted to throw the pack down. We shared one sleeping bag to reduce weight and carried no tent. I carried a smaller day pack with food and a cook pot, but I didn't think he would ever backpack again. Luckily, as in the words of John Muir, "the mountains were calling," and it wasn't long before we ordered another Kelty pack for me, and we never stopped backpacking together until many years and miles later. I still have my original pack, sadly no longer used, but well worn from many good backcountry trips.

In the future, we would drop the packs in a basecamp and climb up the Lyell Glacier in Yosemite to the summit of Mount Lyell. We were learning that breathtaking, 360-degree rewards were in store for us if we summited these fantastic high-altitude peaks. We also became acquainted with the tiny rewards of high-altitude plants and flowers clinging to outcroppings high above timberline. Also in Yosemite high country, we climbed Mount Dana from Tuolumne Pass and looked thousands of feet down to Mono Lake and the Mono Craters to the east. Another time we crossed Vogelsang Pass, left our packs, and summited Vogelsang Peak looking down to the west following the tributaries of the Merced River flowing to Yosemite Valley. Further south in the Ritter Range, we camped at Thousand Island Lake, arose early, and climbed Banner Peak which towers above the lake. With our youthful energy after that climb, we hiked all the way out to the June Lake loop by moonlight to our VW van, many miles downhill. On different trips, we attempted to summit Mount Ritter, once from the west over Hemlock Crossing at the San Joaquin River, but finally made the summit on a snowy climb from Lake Ediza on the east side. I really struggled on that climb, sinking through the snow, but after making the summit, we had an exhilarating descent, glissading much of the way down on the snow using our ice axes for brakes. In northern Yosemite National Park, on another trip we climbed Matterhorn Peak in the Sawtooth Range near Bridgeport, California. Nearing the top, when we were struggling up a huge talus slope, a jet plane flew level with us and tipped his wings; I could see the pilot wave, but he was flying so fast, I hadn't even heard the plane approach. These were all difficult climbs ranging in altitude from twelve thousand to thirteen thousand feet, but not technical, though we sometimes carried a rope for safety in steep ascents. We were always very careful about timing and weather, rising early and turning back if weather or time threatened. We respected the code of good climbing, always putting safety first.

In the fall of 1967, Wes was hired by Death Valley National Monument (now Park) for a seasonal naturalist position. I ended up working part-time for the Natural History Association, learning photography and darkroom skills. The season there runs from October to April each year, though permanent employees live and work there all year, even during the hottest summer months. Wes was hired for the cooler, busy season, and we looked forward to the new adventure.

When we arrived in Death Valley, we were assigned to a small studio apartment in the employees' housing area in Cow Hollow. Our neighbor on one side was Bob Krear, twenty years older than we, and a seasoned mountaineer who had been in the Tenth Mountain Infantry Division in Italy in World War II. He had a PhD in animal behavior and ecology from the University of Colorado and had worked seasonally in many national parks. Bob was an excellent hiker, scientist, and naturalist. He never generalized without knowing the facts. From Bob, I learned to really look carefully for wildlife. He had done his PhD on the behavior of the Rocky Mountain pika, a small furry member of the lagomorph (rabbit) family. When we hiked with Bob, he always paused near the top and said, "We go together to the summit." He was a bachelor and an excellent cook, having cooked for himself and the Murie expedition to the Arctic in the 1950s. (The Murie brothers were biologists known primarily for their studies of wildlife—Olaus for the elk in Jackson Hole, Wyoming, and his brother, Adolph, for the wolves of Mount McKinley/Denali in Alaska.) Bob taught me how to make lasagna and many other items, some of which he had learned from Mardy Murie in Jackson Hole, Wyoming, where he was an adopted member of the Murie family. We three became good friends, and I knew him for fifty years until his death at age ninety-five in December 2017 when I was seventy-four. From the time of his retirement at sixty-five, he lived alone in his cabin in Estes Park, Colorado, at Rocky Mountain National Park. I was a guest there many times, and only three years before his death did he let me cook for him instead of he cooking for me and my husband. One morning at breakfast, he asked, "Do you know *how* to cook an egg?" At sixty-two, I thought he was kidding me, but he was serious and proceeded to say, "Start with a very hot pan!" He knew how to cook!

Another friend in Death Valley was Sharon Gerhardt. Sharon; her husband, Bob; and two-year-old son, Mike, lived down the hill from us. Bob was a seasonal ranger for the park. Sharon and I spent many hours hiking and enjoying conversation over peppermint tea. She also encouraged me to order crunchy granola which was a new breakfast product then. We shared many recipes, some of which I have today. I was impressed with Sharon's outdoor skills, which included carrying her son on her back for long hikes. I was twenty-four then and starting to wish I could combine parenting with an outdoor life—and beginning to realize that Wes probably didn't want children. One time Sharon and I climbed Corkscrew Peak (with Mike in the pack) scouting a route and following rock cairns all the way up. I found an ancient chert spearpoint halfway up the slopes. As it clouded over and threatened rain, unusual for Death Valley, it was Sharon who quickly advised us to get down off the summit and out of the danger of lightning. She and I have only seen each other twice since then, but have shared Christmas cards every year. She is now divorced and lives in Washington State, still leading an active life. She worked many years scheduling for Camp Denali at Wonder Lake in Denali National Park.

In Death Valley that year, we also became good friends with Edward and Judy Abbey. Ed was a published writer (*Fire on the Mountain*, 1962) but not well known yet, and we were amused by his dry remarks, stories of river running, and his critical jokes about the National Park Service. He had previously worked at Arches National Park as a backcountry ranger and was writing a book about it. He had applied for a ranger position at Death Valley, but had been turned down, he thought because of his beard and his developing reputation as an anarchist. His wife, Judy, however, was hired to teach elementary classes at the small school in Death Valley. She taught the children of park service employees and the Shoshone Indian Reservation. Ed drove the school bus an hour each way to and from the town of Shoshone outside the park each day. He was entrusted with the middle and high school kids who attended school there.

Ed and Wes did some grueling hikes together, and the four of us occasionally shared dinners. One evening at their small park service house, I recall Ed sitting on the floor in a long kayak that he was preparing for a river run somewhere in the Southwest. Memorably, I cooked for them in our studio apartment on Ed's fortieth birthday. Ed and Wes had been a good intellectual match for each other, and at the end of the season, when Wes and I were about to depart from Death Valley, Ed walked up to our VW bus with a gift of a dry salami rolled up in a *New York Review of Books*. I remember him waving goodbye, wearing his signature red bandana around his neck. I never saw Ed again, but two summers later, when we were living at Glacier Bay National Monument, he sent us his newly published book, *Desert Solitaire*. I sat in our rustic island cabin, warmed by an oil stove, reading that impressive book, and when I put it down, I said out loud to myself, "You have really done it now, Ed!" I was right; he went on to become famous.

Wes had two days off a week, and we usually took off in the VW to find a hiking route. There weren't too many established trails in Death Valley, but there were many old mines, elusive springs, and old routes established by the early prospectors. We also climbed many of the peaks surrounding the valley—Telescope, Navares, Thimble, Waghaui, Grapevine, and Pyramid Peaks. We scouted out old miners who were legendary and still living then. We found Seldom Seen Slim (very dirty) living in a trailer in Ballarat. We spent one whole rainy afternoon over tea listening to stories by Panamint Russ and the Andersons in their cabins way out in Butte Valley. Another time I ran into the legendary Panamint Annie in the grocery store in Beatty, and she announced to me, "I am Panamint Annie, and I've been here longer than anybody." She looked like it too by then—beautifully weathered with old age and wearing a huge sun hat.

We hiked into Hungry Bill's Ranch, which was just an old ruin of rock walls and fruit trees. Other mines we visited were in the north near the Racetrack—probably named from the rocks seemingly pushed across by heavy winds over the slick muddy playa. We saw Teakettle Junction, the Lost Burro Mine, and the Hunter Cabin, where we spent a cold night cooking porterhouse steaks on a woodstove with another ranger and his wife. The next morning, we woke to several inches of snow and got out with a four-wheel-drive patrol vehicle.

At the end of that season, in the spring of 1967, we moved to the South Rim of the Grand Canyon where Wes would attend the Albright Training Center in preparation for becoming a permanent naturalist with the National Park Service. We had both thought a life living and working in the national parks might suit us. A couple of months later, however, we could see the expectations and conflicts that we might run into in that structured atmosphere. Then, when they assigned Wes to a position as a ranger on boat patrol in the Everglades, far from mountains and deserts that we both loved, he decided against being a permanent employee. He resigned and arranged for another seasonal job that coming summer in Olympic National Park in Washington. While at Grand Canyon, we hiked every chance we got, dropping over the rim with backpacks and hiking to and from the river on many of the unmaintained trails (Hance, Grandview, Bass, Tanner). At that time, these trails had not been traveled much since mining days, and they were pretty rough. We heard about

Harvey Butchart, a mathematician from Flagstaff, who was notorious for his solo canyon hiking. People often read a small book he had published about the old mining trails and routes. Schooled in geology, Wes had excellent skill with reading topographic maps; in addition, we followed rock cairns, where they existed, in order to find our way. In places, we had to lower ourselves down crumbling rock ledges to reach the level below, but we were strong and careful. We also hiked up and down the well-traveled Kaibab and Bright Angel Trails, even making that trip to and from the river once in one day, covering a distance of twenty miles and an elevation change of five thousand feet. Another time, I hiked with two other women for three days along the Tonto Plateau from Pipe Springs to the Bright Angel Trail and up to the rim. By the time Wes and I left the Grand Canyon late that spring, we were completely infatuated with the place—the views, smells and descending sounds of the canyon wrens. We would return several times.

In the summer of 1967, the Summer of Love in Haight-Ashbury in San Francisco, we went to live in Olympic National Park in Washington State where we were stationed at Staircase Rapid. Our housing was a delightful traditional white canvas tent cabin on a wooden platform, complete with a woodstove, bureau, bookshelf, and bed. Light was from candles or lanterns, and we had a Coleman gas stove for cooking when we didn't want to fire up the woodstove. I loved the woodstove, however, and remember picking blackberries and baking pies that summer. We showered outdoors in a tarp shelter with a bucket and used an outhouse. The tent cabin was in the lush alder woods near a stream away from the buildings, and we had complete privacy. It was a hot summer, so we welcomed the shade over our tent.

One of the rangers, who had trained with Wes at Grand Canyon that spring, was starting his permanent position there and lived in the ranger station. Our friend, Bob Krear, was stationed for the summer at the northern end of the park at Sol Duc Hot Springs. We met him a few times for hikes in the rainforest, and he pointed out edible mushrooms and fascinating slime molds that moved. Wes and I hiked all over the park that summer and climbed the glacier slopes of Mount Olympus with the Seattle Mountaineers. When Wes was working, I had many hours to myself and continued my photography in the lush woods. At the end of the summer, Wes needed to stay longer, so I rode a Greyhound bus to Berkeley to find an apartment and a job so he could return to grad school in political science. On campus, I got a job in the History Department in the graduate secretary's office assisting students with records and information. Luckily, I also found a large affordable flat for one hundred dollars a month on the north side of campus at 2476 Hilgard Avenue.

We settled in Berkeley for the fall and winter of 1967/68. These were turbulent times in Berkeley. In the midsixties, UC had been the site of the FSM (Free Speech Movement) with Mario Savio and others protesting on campus. Again, when we came there to live, there were protests and riots against the Vietnam War and the Cambodian situation. Often, there was tear gas on campus and windows broken on Telegraph Avenue. Later came the Peoples' Park Protest when the university wanted to build dorms on a piece of their land that had been a community garden for several years.

Meanwhile, Wes decided to quit grad school and get a research job on campus instead. He encouraged me to transfer my credits, enroll at Berkeley, and finish my BA degree in design where I emphasized ceramics and photography. At our flat, I blacked out the kitchen windows and set up a removable darkroom. Jim Morley, from Muir Woods days, encouraged my photography and took me to Gasser's photo shop in San Francisco to help me purchase a good lens for my enlarger. Everyone there knew him, and they treated me well, packing up quite a few items at a good price. I am still reluctant to part with that treasured Fujinon enlarger lens and some of the darkroom equipment we purchased that day. By this time, I had accumulated many negatives from the national parks and trails and also started doing student work of still life vegetables and eggs in the apartment living room. By the time I finished my degree a couple of years later, I was more interested in pursuing photography than ceramics.

In the spring of 1968, Wes and a high school friend, Jack Fulton, returned to Grand Canyon. They hiked from the remote Indian village of Supai to the Little Colorado River—a monthlong cross-country trip with few trails from west to east. Prior to leaving on the trip, Wes did hours of research and studied with Otis "Dock" Marston, a well-known "canyoneer," who had accumulated a huge basement archive of Grand Canyon material in his Berkeley home. Wes also met Colin Fletcher, who had made a similar trip and written a book called *The Man Who Walked through Time*.

Wes's hike with Jack was quite a feat, requiring research, mapping, and both mental and physical stamina. Prior to their hike, I went to Grand Canyon with them to help place two food caches they could access during the hike. In March 1968, we celebrated my twenty-fifth birthday on the trail, eating Logan bread, a nutritious backpacking food that I had baked. We descended all day on a beautiful but rough trail and hid one cache just above river level near Tanner Rapid. There, we were lucky to hitch a raft ride with Hatch River Expeditions to Phantom Ranch downstream and hike out the well-traveled Bright Angel Trail instead of back up the Tanner Trail. A couple of days later, we hid the other cache in a remote place below the rim near Apache Point to the west.

After saying goodbye to Wes and Jack near Supai and Topacopa Hilltop, I drove home in the VW bus to return to school. At that time, I had never driven alone on a long-distance trip. Bravely, I drove east for a few hours on a long dirt road to the Grand Canyon Village and park service headquarters at the South Rim. There, I checked in at the ranger station, as prearranged, so they would know the long hike had started and that I was safely out of the backcountry. Then I went south from the canyon to Route 66 at Williams, Arizona, and headed west across the Mojave Desert. In Amboy, I pulled over to stay in a motel, but hardly slept, thinking of the movie *Psycho* and its famous murder in the Bates Motel.

I felt very alone, got up the next morning, shyly ate breakfast at the adjoining café, and continued all the way to Berkeley. There was no interstate then, just an undivided highway. Arriving late afternoon, I was relieved and shaking from road miles when I got out of the VW after parking it safely behind our apartment. (Recently, in 2016 we all got together with Tom Martin of Vishnu Temple Press to revisit Wes and Jack's hike through pictures and Jack's movie. Tom and Wes have now meticulously edited and transcribed the journal that Wes kept during that hike in 1968, and it is in the archives of Grand Canyon National Park. Now, we are all still in touch and have reached the fiftieth anniversary of the hike, and see it as an accomplishment to look back on.)

Before the hike, Wes had arranged for another seasonal naturalist position for the summer of 1968—this time at Glacier Bay National Monument in Southeast Alaska. Because I was finishing my semester, I flew up a month later. Martin Luther King Jr. had been shot in April, and then Robert Kennedy was shot two months later, on June 5, 1968, when I was studying for finals in Berkeley. I was really moved and saddened by this unusual violence in our country. Wes remembers lowering the flag at remote Glacier Bay that day.

When I finally got to Glacier Bay, we lived in the Lagoon Island Cabin, and I waitressed at the Glacier Bay Lodge. Many years before, the cabin had been moved to the small island from a navy base in nearby Gustavus and was set up as the first headquarters of Glacier Bay National Monument. When we got there, it hadn't been inhabited for a few years, but we wanted the wilderness experience when it was offered to us for the summer. They had cleaned the small three-room cabin and installed an oil-burning stove, a water cistern for collecting rainfall, a sink with one faucet, beds and a table with chairs. The trail to the outhouse was carpeted with moss through a grove of Sitka spruce, and fireweed bloomed pink along the rocky shoreline in early summer. All of this had a view across the bay to the towering, ice-covered Fairweather Range. Wes and I each had a small rowboat for getting to and from shore to the headquarters and lodge. We lived in brown rubber boots that summer, otherwise known as "Sitka tennis shoes."

Friends there were Greg and Barbara Streveler whom we had known at the Albright Training Center at Grand Canyon. With Barbara, I worked in a garden she planted each year in nearby Gustavus, growing huge strawberries and cabbages in the short growing season with long daylight hours. She also taught me how to smoke salmon, which we took on our camping trips. She was expecting her second child and flew out by a seaplane, known as "The Goose," to stay in Juneau near the hospital before her delivery date. A few weeks later, she and Greg returned with the new baby. I was learning that families thrived and coped with many challenges living in national parks.

Wes had a spectacular job working most days on the tour boat, the *Seacrest*, that cruised up and down the bay to the Muir Glacier with park naturalists interpreting the scenery. On days off, we often had the boat drop us off with our backpacks on small islands or in coves near the glaciers. We explored on foot, and the boat picked us up the next day as arranged. Park visitors on the boat couldn't believe we had been out there camping and roaming around in the wilderness "with the bears!" We saw a few black bears, but we called out when hiking, “Hi, bear! Go, bear!” and we never had a risky encounter.

Luckily, it was light most of the night in Southeast Alaska in the summer. When not on the bay, we canoed to ruins of an old fox farm, climbed on glaciers, and did some fishing. When my parents visited, the lodge owner took us on a guided trip in a small cabin cruiser with Harold Bradley, a former president of the Sierra Club, and his wife. He was ninety and yodeled across the sound with a booming voice. Another time, on a rainy day, my father and I went fishing in my rowboat offshore. We hadn’t been hunkered down long in our raincoats when I caught a huge halibut, and my father happily said, “Well, Nance, we can go in now!” We ate fresh halibut with homegrown cabbage for several days in our cozy cabin.

In August that summer, Wes’s younger brother Bruce came to be a deckhand on the *Seacrest.* He lived with us in the three-room cabin, and we had a lot of fun hiking around the island during midnight sunsets and mucking around on the shoreline in our boots. When Wes and I left at the end of the season, Bruce remained for another few weeks, and he even returned for a second season the following summer. With its many inlets and high glaciated mountains, Glacier Bay is a spectacular place. My daughter and family visited there in 2013, following in my footsteps, to see “Grandma’s cabin” across the lagoon, and connected me with the current park service employees who welcomed my story about the Lagoon Island Cabin.

Back in Berkeley in the fall of 1968, I continued school and finished my coursework in design in June 1969. I didn’t attend the graduation because (happily) we were hiking in the Sierra. During that year, Wes worked as a researcher in the political science department on campus and continued his Grand Canyon research and friendship with Dock Marston. During the summer of 1969, when we stayed in Berkeley, the United States landed on the moon on July 20. When they landed, I was walking across the UC Berkeley campus near the Campanile when suddenly the bells rang out with a wonderful medley of moon songs, “Moon River,” “My Love Is the Man in the Moon,” “Blue Moon,” and several others. Complete strangers were smiling and greeting each other as they milled around. That evening, in our apartment, we tried to focus our eyes on a weak, blurry television transmission of the now-famous moon walk. It was an amazing event to experience.

In September 1969, we went down the Colorado River in the Grand Canyon with Dock Marston who was seventy-five at the time. Beforehand, we had the unusual treat of driving with Dock all night in our VW bus from Berkeley to the Las Vegas airport where we would catch a small flight to Lee's Ferry and meet the boating party. On the drive, Dock talked about river history the whole way. I was sandwiched between Wes and Dock in the front seat, and I thought for sure he would want to crawl in the back and sleep on the mattress, but I was impressed that he never stopped talking all night. His enthusiasm was infectious, and we felt very lucky to hear his wealth of river stories. As Tom Martin, Dock's biographer, many years later would say, "Wow, an all-nighter through the Mojave Desert with Dock Marston. I am envious!"

On the river, I took about eighty black-and-white, medium-format photos that turned out well considering the fact that I had been photographing and doing my own darkroom work for only about a year. (Those negatives are now in the archive of Grand Canyon National Park.) Wes and I were able to go nearly free on this experimental boat, owned by Jim Bob Rowland, if we cooked and acted as deckhands. It was a trip of a lifetime, as it turned out, because it was one of the last hard-hull motor trips permitted through Grand Canyon National Park. Most trips allowed today are in rubber rafts, kayaks, and wooden rowboats, which must limit motor use. Ours was a fast trip (only five days), and I rather envied the quieter, slower float trips that we passed. They were surprised to see us with one unusual motorboat and only seven passengers.

Years later, in July 2016, we met with Tom Martin who was interested in our photos and oral history of that remarkable trip for both his Marston biography and for the Grand Canyon National Park records. In addition, it turned out that my father had known Otis "Dock" Marston in Berkeley in the 1930s when his parents rented a house from him on Vine Street, and he was a student at Cal. My dad remembered gardening for Marston and swimming in his pool. They got to meet and reminisce again at a dinner we arranged at our apartment in Berkeley.

In the fall of 1969, Wes and I returned for another winter season in Death Valley. He was a naturalist again, giving evening slideshows and short nature walks and answering questions behind the information desk at the museum. I worked for the Natural History Association again, sorting their photo files and assisting behind the front desk during heavy visitation. One time when I showed up for work, I was told to go home and change out of my bright-yellow short dress for something more conservative. Miniskirts were the fashion then, but not with the National Park Service meeting the public! (These days, they have uniforms for volunteers.)

A few weeks before our arrival, the Tate-La Bianca murders had occurred in the Los Angeles area. Charles Manson and his family of followers had hidden out in Goler Wash southwest of Mengel Pass in the Death Valley area. They were arrested and jailed in Inyo County by a law enforcement group that included county and park service officers. By the time we arrived in October, this was still big news. Manson and a few were still in jail in Independence, but officials had released some of the group for whom they didn't have enough proof to keep behind bars. Those stragglers dispersed, or so the officials thought.

Not long after arriving in Death Valley, Wes and I started our exploratory hikes again. One of our first hikes that fall was to be an overnight backpack trip to Panamint City, an abandoned mining town on the east side of Death Valley. We would camp there for the night and continue the next day to climb Sentinel Peak, which sat on the ridge and overlooked Death Valley from the west. We drove around to the old mining town of Ballarat and north to the old dirt road in the direction of Panamint City. We knew the road had been washed out in a flash flood a couple of years before, so we parked the car and hiked up the steep old road toward the mining town, which we expected to be empty. (We had stayed there a couple of years before.)

When we leveled out in the valley approaching the old town, we noticed peace symbols and other marks spray-painted on the boulders along the road. Almost immediately, we heard gunshots and bullets zoom over our heads. We thought someone must be practice shooting, and we shouted out, but as soon as we stepped forward, the bullets went overhead again, too close. Someone was warning us to stay out. Understandably, I was terrified and wanted to head back to the VW, but Wes thought we could angle away and go up into the trees to camp, continue the next day, bypassing Panamint City on the hillside above, and on to Sentinel Peak.

Almost over my dead body, that's what we did. I never slept a wink in the woods that night, thinking that every tiny sound I heard was someone approaching in the dark.

The next day we hiked higher and looked down with a telephoto lens on several people milling around Panamint City. We made our climb of the peak, descended back to our car, and drove into Owens Valley to buy groceries before backtracking to Death Valley headquarters. When in Independence, the Inyo County seat, we reported the shooting to the sheriff. They didn't take the report seriously that day, but noted it and, within a week, were in Furnace Creek, questioning Wes again. Eventually, they searched and found that the released Manson Family members were the ones encamped in Panamint City, shooting at us. That was a close call I have never forgotten.

In the fall of 1969, I finally received my BA degree in design in the mail at the Furnace Creek Post Office in Death Valley. The diploma was signed by Ronald Reagan, then the governor of California. Not being a Reagan supporter, I found that amusing. It had taken me eight years to complete my degree, delayed by many trips and park service adventures, but it was certainly worth the wait.

We continued exploring that fall and winter, enjoying different parts of the valley—the Pupfish Marsh, Pyramid Peak, and Echo Canyon with the geologist Jim McAllister. He lived in a trailer at that time out on Highway 127 east of the park and one night took us to Tecopa Hot Springs. It was a clean, well-kept indoor building with separate sides for men and women. There was also a senior mobile home park nearby; I was young and got an eyeful of older women's bodies that night. I came back out to the VW with many comments for Wes and Jim. Funny to think of it today. Did I think I would never get that old?

We met another geologist, Mitch Reynolds, that season who was from UC Berkeley. He was camping with his wife and young family, and we brought them all home for baths and dinner. Both of these geologists encouraged Wes to apply for graduate school in geology at Berkeley. After his acceptance, we moved back to Berkeley for the fall of 1970, and this time, Wes thrived on the graduate work in a field he loved.

About a year and a half later, Wes completed his coursework and passed his orals. To support this effort, I had taken a job on the Berkeley campus, this time a full-time job as the undergraduate secretary in the math department. It was a good desk job assisting undergraduates with course planning and records, and I also made friends who gave me a social life. This time Wes and I lived in a nice apartment on Prospect Street near the Memorial Stadium. In the same complex, we became friends with another geology graduate student, Julie Donnelly, and her partner, Steve Silverstein, a dentist. By this time, with Wes's encouragement, I had started running on the track and had purchased my first pair of running shoes—bright-red, three-stripe Adidas. Julie and I became good friends and started running together, meeting every morning at six o'clock for a three-mile run up and back in Strawberry Canyon. By the time I reported to work each day, I had run three miles, showered, dressed, and walked to work on campus. We were young, and we were fit. Julie and I were also reliable and committed. It was a friendship and running partnership that would continue on and off for several years.

During Christmas break in December 1970, Wes, Larry Jager (a Mill Valley friend), and I flew to Mexico to climb the big volcanoes Popocatepetl and Orizaba, one slightly less and one over eighteen thousand feet. We had to plan well for this trip. Each climb was a long day that started in the wee hours, making the ascents with crampons on ice as the sun was coming up, and the descent in the afternoons when the snow was softer so we could safely glissade down with ice axes. The climbs each started from hikers' huts at about fourteen to fifteen thousand feet, so altitude was already a challenge for sleeping. The climbs were done without oxygen and were very slow—one foot in front of the other with lots of pauses for breathing. The slopes were steep but not unsafe if you were careful, and in a few places, we roped up to get around crevasses. I did quite well with the altitude, no altitude sickness other than a headache. The feeling of accomplishment has stayed with me all my life. The sun was bright, and the views from the top were spectacular. Again, I was discovering that as hard as it was, there were rewards at the top of a mountain.

As we turned the corner into 1971, Wes and I stayed in Berkeley and he continued the grueling hours of study toward his PhD. This was a tough time for us both. I continued working at the math department and spent many weekends in Mill Valley with my parents, where I enjoyed a relaxing atmosphere in my old hometown. I again enjoyed gardening and picking out plants at the nursery with my dad. By this time, they lived at 114 Sunnyside Avenue, within walking distance to town.

In the spring of 1971, my father was having angina pains and was admitted to Marin General Hospital in early March. After a brief stay, he was sent home with guidelines for care through diet and exercise. Later that year in October, at age fifty-nine, he was admitted again to the hospital and then transported to Presbyterian Hospital in San Francisco where they quickly prepared him for open-heart surgery on November 17, 1971. Surgery of this type was not common then, but he survived it well. During the surgery, I waited with my mother at their home in Mill Valley. While she sat nearby on the porch, I chose to weed in the garden all day—a symbolic gesture of love for my father, knowing that he took pride in his garden. We were greatly relieved to receive the phone call that afternoon saying he was out of surgery. In a couple of days, we were able to visit him, see his chest staples and smiles. Ten days later, he was home. For years thereafter, he was devoted to his exercise program each morning and was careful about what he ate, knowing that he couldn't tolerate high fat and cholesterol.

In the fall of 1971, after Wes finished coursework and passed his orals, we started making plans for where he would do fieldwork. The first suggestion was to work in Africa at Olduvai Gorge near the Leakeys and their team, but it was soon considered politically unsafe, so we settled on returning to Death Valley where we would set up a field camp of our own. Friends and family couldn't believe that we were going to live in a tent. With my camping experience, that idea didn't bother me, but we were actually able to rent a cabin in Wildrose Canyon from the park service. We lived there for a short time, but ultimately things didn't work out because of many stresses on our relationship that occurred then and had been building up over time. I left Death Valley, and Wes eventually left also.

One might think that a marriage with this amount of adventure and shared experience would last, but Wes and I eventually reached a serious fork in the road. For some time, I had been wanting to address my more feminine instincts; I wanted a home and family and a stronger recognition of my needs. I loved outdoor adventures, but maybe I had climbed enough mountains and needed to grow in my own direction. Having a home and family would have compromised Wes's needs for unburdened research and adventure. I had participated in nearly every hike, climb, and challenge with him and even enjoyed long-distance running, but he emotionally could not participate in what I needed, and our personalities were very different.

The writing had been on the wall for some time. We both recognized, even then, that he could not, and should not, compromise what mattered most to him and that I could not either. Parting was messy and tough. New relationships did not work out for either of us for some time. We needed space and time for growth apart. We split quickly, and the adjustment came slowly and painfully. In the long run, we made the right decision, and the divorce became final in 1973 when I was thirty. Many years later, he thanked me "for putting a pack on his back" and admitted we had worked on his issues more than mine. Still today, I treasure my memories with him and of living in national parks, pushing myself to achieve goals I could not have imagined before. I now recognized a need in myself to have a life that always included outdoor experiences and challenges, as well as home and travel.

Wes continued doing research in geology, though not in Death Valley at that time. He finished his PhD at Berkeley, eventually married fellow grad student Gail Mahood, who became a geology professor at Stanford. Wes has had a distinguished career at the USGS in Menlo Park, California, and has had several research areas in Chile, Alaska, Death Valley, the Eastern Sierra, Oregon, and Washington State. We meet occasionally at high school reunions, memorials, and his geo-birthday events he hosts for friends, colleagues, and family. These events have been at his research areas in Washington State, Katmai National Park in Alaska, and Mammoth Lakes, California.

I went on to do graduate work at Berkeley for an MA in design, emphasizing photography. My photographic thesis of sixty black-and-white photos of Owens Valley, California, took me back to a familiar area in the Eastern Sierra which I loved. *The Land of Little Rain*, by Mary Austin and *Deepest Valley* by Genny Schumacher Smith became my Bibles. Eventually, I became a pretty good navigator in my own right.

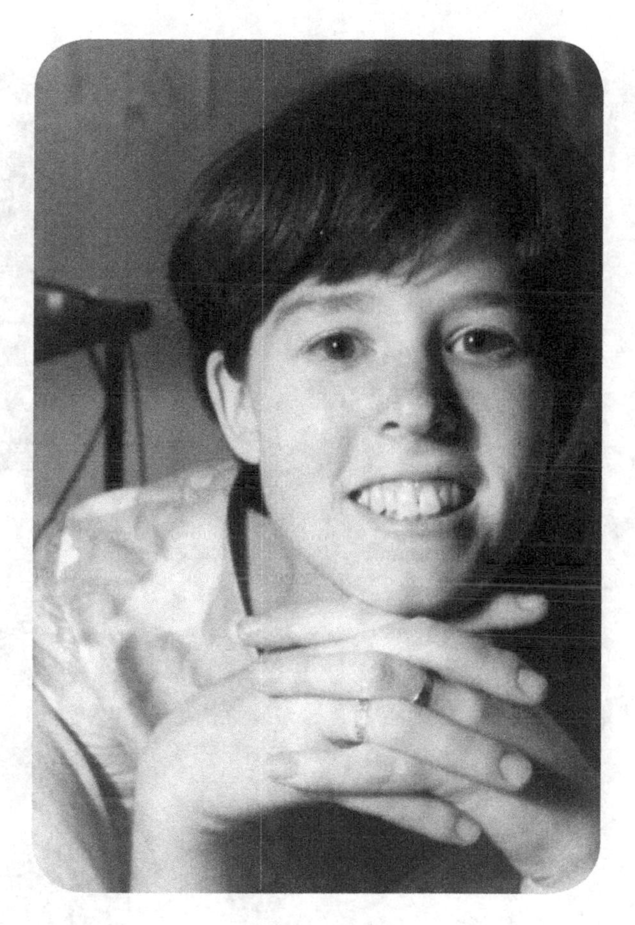

Nancy, 1965

Wes Hildreth running Dipsea Trail, Stinson Beach, California, 1965

Nancy at Hemlock Crossing, Sierra Nevada, on the way to climb Mt. Ritter from the west

Wes with Justice William O. Douglas and his wife Cathy in Muir Woods National Monument in 1966. (Photo by author)

Wes at Borax Gardens in Death Valley National Monument, winter 1967

Wes and Nancy in Death Valley National Monument, Christmas photo 1967 that said "Greetings from Death Valley!

Nancy and Wes at Glacier Bay National Monument, Alaska, 1968

Nancy and Wes at Lagoon Island Cabin, Glacier Bay National Monument, summer 1968

Wes, Nancy, and Larry Jager on summit of
Popocatepetl (17,805 ft.), December 1970

Wes and Richard Delgado in motion

CHAPTER 3

A Fork in the Trail

In 1973, I tried another administrative job on the Berkeley campus, but I had made a poor choice of boring, statistical work, and I felt very lonely in an isolated office. I missed my former outdoor life and spent a lot of time staring out the window, wishing I were outside. I kept my spirits up by running every day at lunchtime on the campus sports fields with my close friend Julie Donnelly. In a few months, another friend, Diane Fulton from Marin County, was leaving a job at Judges and Spares Restaurant in Point Richmond and recommended me to Al Brennan, the owner. Al and his partner, Don, were wonderful gay men who had envisioned a café that embodied all that California cuisine was becoming in the Bay Area. With Diane, they had made a cookbook with recipes made from scratch and with the best ingredients they could find. Each day we made fresh herb bread, a main course, special sandwiches, and desserts. We had a rotating schedule so we each got experience at cooking, baking, serving, and cleaning up. The restaurant had a coffeehouse atmosphere, serving lunch and dinner, all at reasonable prices. Al used to say he would like everyone to be able to afford a meal at his restaurant even if it was just soup and salad.

In the artistic community of Point Richmond on San Francisco Bay, the clientele came from the local area but also Marin County and the East Bay. The word got out, and soon there was a good following. Most of the employees lived nearby, but I traveled from Albany, where I was living alone in a cute basement apartment at 1602 Marin Avenue. Since I lived near Berkeley, Al would often ask me to pick up produce from the Monterey Market and items from the Cheese Board. Both were in the area of Shattuck Avenue that became known as the Gourmet Ghetto and included the original Peet's Coffee on Vine Street and Alice Water's Chez Panisse Restaurant on Shattuck Avenue. Al always loaded me up with food from our restaurant to take home since I commuted, and the other employees were encouraged to eat their meals there as part of their pay.

When I was at work, I chowed down on cheese or carrot cake for breakfast, as well as sandwiches and main course delicacies. I was thin and never gained an ounce working so hard, and I loved the lively, somewhat offbeat atmosphere. We were a family of friends—Zander, Miles, "Turtle" (all three Al's sons), Frank, Wendy, Lucrecia, and many more, working various shifts. Sometimes my shift at the restaurant started at six in the morning making multiple loaves of herb bread for the day, along with cheesecake, linzer torte, carrot cake, or crème caramel, just to name a few. A couple of hours later someone else would arrive to start making the main course and the sandwich choices. Right from the beginning, Al put me in charge on Friday nights. I can still remember him calling throughout the kitchen area, "Clean up after yourselves! Do your own dishes! All anyone needs for cooking is a good kitchen knife!" and shouting, "Nancy just tried to turn the shrimp creole into spaghetti sauce!" when I added too much tomato sauce on my first Friday.

During the summer of 1974, we cooked and listened to the radio all day to follow the Watergate hearings in Washington, DC. None of us had ever experienced anything like it, and it was fascinating and discouraging. The radio was centrally located, and we would catch bits and pieces as we scurried around cooking, cleaning up, and serving out front.

At first I worked full-time at the restaurant but soon was accepted to graduate school at Berkeley for an MA in design, specializing in photography. It turned out that Wendy Niles, my friend at the restaurant, was also accepted to the same program but in textile arts. We would become very good friends, even traveling together to Owens Valley, where I was photographing for my thesis, and in later years to Capitol Reef National Park in Utah. After a few months of graduate school, I had to reduce my work hours at the restaurant, and eventually I left and worked part-time instead in a photo lab on campus.

We all loved Al and Don, the owners of the restaurant. They were colorful and caring. Once when I was upset over a relationship, Al came to my apartment bearing food and kind words. I was always comfortable talking to him. But Al and Don eventually sold the restaurant because of Al's poor health, and a group of employees kept it running for a few years thereafter. They asked me if I wanted to join in ownership, but I declined. I loved working there with my newfound friends, but I had different ambitions.

In graduate school at Berkeley, I took many classes in photography and design. The two photography instructors were Penny D'haemers and William Garnett. The classes were varied and always involved critiques and discussion. One time we had a small seminar with Ansel Adams, who displayed his famous photograph of Mount Whitney with the Alabama Hills in the foreground. Other times we traveled to Big Sur and visited the home studios of Brett Weston and Morley Baer. I was surrounded by a compatible group of students with whom I often took photo field trips. One time when camping with this group in Big Sur, we had wine with dinner and my friends commented that I was the only one who knew how to put up a tent in the dark even though I was as tipsy as the rest of them.

Some of us had part-time jobs assisting students in the photo lab in the College of Environmental Design. There we taught basic film and printing techniques to the students studying architecture, landscape architecture, and city planning. By this time, I felt confident teaching photography and enjoyed working with students in the darkroom. When it came time for me to choose an area for my thesis, I chose the beautiful rural Owens Valley, just east of the mountainous Sierra Nevada. I had been there many times when I lived in Death Valley and already had a fondness for the area. I began that project after my coursework in 1974, completing in the fall of 1975. When the weather was good, I traveled to Owens Valley, which was eight hours away—sometimes alone but occasionally with fellow students.

Since my divorce from Wes, I had dated a few people but had not developed any deep attachments. This was a time of transition for me. I enjoyed renewing old friendships, especially with my childhood friend Suzy (Rosse) McCulloch, who was now living in Albany with her husband, Chuck. They were creative and lighthearted and invited me to live with them for a couple of months while I got resettled in Berkeley. Then, for the first time, I ended up living alone in an apartment. That felt very strange, but I gradually learned to eat meals alone and get accustomed to the quiet evenings. During the winters I went on local Sierra Club hikes, and in the summers I went on beautiful backpacking trips with friends in the Sierra—once to Red Peak Pass, another time near Sonora Pass, and also multiday loop trips over Muir and Mather Passes. One summer I visited my Park Service friends Fred and Mary Ellen Ackerman in Death Valley. They picked me up in Owens Valley and drove me out to 124-degree weather where we spent our time indoors in air-conditioning. They had a new baby, and I ventured outside to hang the diapers on the line, only to take them down because they dried in the hot wind by the time I was finished hanging them up. I had spent three winters in Death Valley but had never experienced that side of Park Service life. Mary Ellen and I also made a dozen apple pies for her freezer that week because someone from nearby Beatty, Nevada, had brought her a huge box of homegrown apples.

By this time, happily, Jerry Marsden had come into my life. When I met Jerry, he always said if he hadn't been a mathematician, he would have been a weatherman or a truck driver. He loved watching clouds and ocean waves and having time to think. In his office at UC Berkeley, where he was a mathematics professor, he had a poster of a gorilla that said, "Sometimes I sits and thinks, and sometimes I just sits." As we got acquainted, he often accompanied me on my photo trips to Owens Valley. He enjoyed just sitting and watching the sky while I put up my tripod and fiddled with my photo equipment. One of my favorite photos is of lenticular clouds caused by high winds; he held the tripod for me that day to keep it from blowing over. Jerry was patient and thoughtful, as well as steadily ambitious about his own career.

Jerry and I had been reintroduced by my friend, Nora Lee, an administrator in the math department. She had hired me for my job there a few years earlier when I was married to Wes and working full-time. I had known Jerry casually when I worked there, and he inquired about me when he heard I was divorced. By this time, he was also divorced. I remembered him as a very kind and warm, friendly person with a nice, quiet sense of humor. He was still a Canadian citizen, but had been hired by UC Berkeley several years earlier after finishing his PhD at Princeton. His undergraduate degree was from the University of Toronto. When we started dating, I was living in an apartment in Albany, and Jerry in a duplex in nearby El Cerrito. It felt natural for me to be with Jerry because of his easygoing nature, and we also shared experiences in the university community where I had spent so much time.

We were very attracted to each other right away. Jerry was a handsome man with big beautiful blue eyes, good features, and a strong build and of medium height. He had won awards as a gymnast in college and enjoyed jogging, tennis, hiking, and skiing. All his adult life, he wore floppy tennis hats to protect his cute bald head, which was fringed with wavy blond hair. Ironically, he had the same August 17 birthday as Wes, but Jerry was only five months older than I, not five years, and they had very different personalities. Jerry and I had a mutual admiration, and it helped that I had more confidence by this time. Pretty quickly, we shared a lot of our feelings, which included the desire to travel, hike, and ski and to have a home and family life someday.

Jerry was already an excellent skier when I met him, but I had been on skis only once or twice. I was eager to learn, and Jerry took on the challenge of teaching me. We often went to Sugar Bowl with another couple, Karen Vogtman and her friend Dan. Jerry and Karen were excellent skiers, but Dan and I were out of control, collapsing all over the bunny slopes and nearly colliding with trees or other skiers. We did catch on after some lessons, and we all eventually went to Mammoth Mountain that spring. Jerry was very patient, and I eventually became a good intermediate skier, but rarely tempted by black diamond runs. In later years, we would buy a ski cabin near Truckee and ski at all the major ski resorts in the Tahoe Basin. We also took up cross-country skiing and snowshoeing, using any excuse to get out in the winter.

Early in our relationship in May 1974, Jerry invited me to spend a month in Paris while he was on sabbatical. It was a wonderful trip, and my first time back in ten years, but this time I was older, thirty-one instead of twenty-one, and more independent. Jerry was working most of the days, but I tucked my Michelin Guide and camera in my backpack and went exploring. I visited museums and many historical sites. I rode the metro and walked from place to place. I reacquainted myself with famous art and photographed in the beautiful parks. Jerry was in residence at a local university but joined me evenings, weekends, and whenever he could. We stayed at a small friendly hotel, the Plaisant Hotel at 50 rue des Bernardins, Paris 5, where we had coffee and croissants each morning on the balcony and enjoyed the cool, sunny May weather. We were serenaded by the sound of police cars each night, the seesawing sound that seemed unique to Paris. While Jerry was at the university, I took French classes daily at Alliance Française in a total immersion program with no spoken English. By the time we left Paris, I was beginning to understand and speak barely enough to order at the outdoor markets and restaurants without just pointing. The month of May was a good time to visit Paris—cool weather, few crowds, and beautiful gardens with early blooms. I found myself blossoming with the flowers and developing a new strength in myself.

That first summer together, when Jerry and I were back in Berkeley, we often drove to Owens Valley in the eastern Sierra so I could photograph. Owens Valley is also known as the "Deepest Valley" in America because it is bordered on each side by mountains—the Sierra Nevada to the west and the White and Inyo Mountains to the east. The valley itself is high desert with grassland and sage covering ancient moraines and volcanic outcroppings. Highway 395 travels through the arid, beautiful valley for about a hundred miles, passing through the towns of Bishop, Big Pine, Independence, and Lone Pine, which sits below Mount Whitney in the south. Jerry had a big car, an Oldsmobile he had jokingly named "Morton." On one of our trips to the valley, we drove his car up to the White Mountains and the bristlecone pines on the east side of Owens Valley where the elevation was well over ten thousand feet. This involved a very steep climb up to Westgard Pass (7,313 ft.) and then north. Morton was not happy making this trip, but we did make it to the Methuselah Grove (9,846 ft.) After visiting the grove of ancient pines (some over four thousand years old), we parked up the road at a gate, and started to hike up the jeep road to the UC White Mountain Research Station on Mount Barcroft (12,470 ft.) just south of White Mountain Peak (14,242 ft.) Soon, an official jeep pulled up alongside and offered us a ride to the station on top. If we wanted to spend a few hours there, the same guy would drive us back down when he descended. We hopped in, rode high above timberline, and had a beautiful day. I got some nice photographs of White Mountain Peak, framed with good summer clouds. After returning to the car, we started our long descent down Westgard Pass. The radiator had boiled over going up the pass, and the automatic transmission gave out going down. Poor Morton had to be towed. We waited a long time for the tow truck to come up from the small town of Big Pine and tow us down the steep road to the repair shop where we ended up spending three days in a motel waiting for the transmission repair. New parts had to be shipped up from Los Angeles. Sadly, Morton was neither a mountain nor a desert car, and we soon replaced him with a used Volkswagen station wagon.

During our first summer together, I also met Jerry's six-year-old son, Christopher, who came on a trip to the Bay Area with Jerry's stepsister, Marilyn. Chris lived with his mother, Jerry's first wife, near Toronto but became a seasoned airline traveler to and from California by the time he was ten. That first summer together, we took Chris camping to Mammoth Lakes and Owens Valley, and I could see how nicely Jerry interacted with him. As I sat outside near the campfire, while Jerry tucked Chris in his sleeping bag in the tent, I overheard singsong stories about "Bobbie the Frog," "Lessons in Life," and whatever else Jerry made up. He was clever and tender with his son and had a good way with children. By this time, I felt that I was in love with a man with whom I could share a good life that might include children. We took short hikes and visited the fish hatchery in Owens Valley, and I taught Chris how to fish in the streams near the campsites where he caught and bravely tasted his first trout.

In the fall and winter of 1974/75, I continued my graduate work in photography while Jerry taught his mathematics classes at Berkeley. We squeezed in a couple of ski trips before Christmas. After Christmas, Jerry had committed to teach in Toronto, where he had been an undergraduate student. Before my classes and job resumed in January, we drove together across the states and north into Canada. On Highway 50 at a pull-out outside Fallon, Nevada, I photographed the VW hubcap encircled with icicles. Jerry was fascinated because he always looked for mathematical reasons for things in nature, which in this case was the result of centrifugal force. He also would see math reasons for swirls in a cup of tea and a few years later would use my photos that showed vectors in cloud formations.

On our trip, the weather was cold, but clear most of the way across the Basin and Range Province in Nevada on "the loneliest highway in America," but well below freezing in Ely, Nevada, where we spent the night in a motel. Walking outside, Jerry shared his experiences of living in below-freezing weather in Toronto—scarf over your face to protect your nostrils and lungs. We continued east where eventually, crossing Nebraska, it was so flat that I read Kurt Vonnegut out loud to Jerry while he drove. Finally, in Canada, I spent a few days with him in Toronto and met his mother, Isobel Phillips, before flying back to continue my studies. I visited again in the spring, and Jerry proposed over ice cream at a small restaurant in Toronto, saying, "I guess we should get married!"

I agreed. "I guess we should!" We were in love and had been having a wonderful time together. We seemed so well suited—our interests and aspirations for our future together. I loved being with Jerry because he was gentle, kind, funny, and very loving. We looked forward to a good future together.

The next summer, Jerry and I were married on July 1, 1975, in Carson City, Nevada, after a backpacking trip to Virginia Lakes in the eastern Sierra. We planned the trip to include the wedding ceremony on our way home because we wanted to keep it simple and celebrate with a party later. Friends had been married there and recommended it instead of Reno for a plain civil ceremony. Jerry focused on that date because, as a Canadian, he would always remember Canada Day also being our wedding anniversary, and he never did forget.

Rufus Bowen (math department) and his wife, Charlie, were with us on the backpack trip, after which we all dressed up and stood together for the ceremony in the judge's cluttered office. Then we attended lunch at South Lake Tahoe where, walking into Harrah's, I put one dollar into the huge Big Bertha slot machine and won a hundred dollars, which paid for a fancy lunch for all of us at the very nice top-floor restaurant overlooking the lake. Jerry reacted to my winnings with his gentle soft humor and laugh followed by "Naaancy!" He loved my luck that day and took it as a good sign for the marriage. Though not a gambler himself, he had math colleagues who were sometimes successful at beating the odds at the tables.

When we returned home to Berkeley, I continued my graduate work, and Jerry went back to work in the math department. That was a lovely summer in Berkeley and on the campus. We were renting a house at 1601 Rose Street and had a large celebration with friends a few weeks later. In those days, we were listening and dancing to the music of the Eagles, the Rolling Stones, Fleetwood Mac, Cat Stevens, and others. We moved the furniture from the bedroom and danced on the hardwood floor; it was a Berkeley party not to be forgotten.

In early September of that year, we traveled through Yosemite over Tioga Pass and down Highway 395 through Owens Valley during a huge rainstorm. At night, the yellow rabbit brush alongside the highway was lit up by lightning. We pulled over briefly and just sat in the car listening and watching, completely surrounded by the storm. Lightning was close but not hitting the valley floor around us, and rain was pounding the roof of the car. By morning it was clear, and Jerry and I started a multiday backpack trip from Onion Valley over Kearsarge Pass (11,760 ft.) to the John Muir Trail and Vidette Meadows and eventually all the way south to Mount Whitney. Jerry and I had a new tepee-style nylon tent we had purchased for a hundred dollars from Sierra Designs when the company was new in Point Richmond. We spent a cozy, dry night while being pounded by another violent summer storm. A few days later, after crossing Forester Pass at 13,153 feet, we camped during a snowstorm and two days later ended up on Mount Whitney (14,496 ft.) on a sunny but cold day. I took a photo of Jerry on the summit in his red ski jacket and floppy hat.

Then we made the long switch-backing descent down to Trail Camp, where we camped for the night, and hiked out to Whitney Portal the next day. We waited a long time trying to hitchhike down to Lone Pine, but finally were picked up by a Forest Service employee who said he was breaking the rules but he would give us a ride. Luckily, he dropped us on Highway 395, and, after the greasy hamburgers and milkshakes that we had been craving, we hitchhiked again in the late afternoon sun going north and eventually back to our parked car at Onion Valley. (These days there are shuttle services for the many hikers who do thru hikes.)

A few weeks later, I discovered I had become pregnant on the trip. I was thirty-two, and we were both eager to have a child. It would be Jerry's second child, but my first. That fall I finished printing photos for my MA photo show to be held in December. I was feeling very sensitive, due to my hormonal changes and all the other pressures, but my photo adviser understood and encouraged me through my tears when I was putting up my show in Wurster Hall. During my studies, she had also warned me about not sharing too many of my ideas with my male colleagues, who had claimed some of my project ideas as their own, and gone out taking photos just where I had. A life lesson well learned about keeping some creative ideas to yourself.

My show on opening night was well attended by friends, fellow students, and faculty. I sold one photo of the Owens River and Mount Tom to a professor from the astronomy department and White Mountain High Altitude Research Station. I wore a long red embroidered Mexican dress over my pregnant tummy and had a wonderful feeling of accomplishment.

From January through June 9, 1976, when Alison was born, I was able to stay at home and could walk, garden, cook, sew, and attend Lamaze classes. I did a limited amount of darkroom work, not wanting to be exposed to the chemicals. Our nice rented house was up the hill above the Monterey Market, a popular produce market in north Berkeley. One morning, Jerry got up to go to work and came back in to tell me he thought the car had been stolen. We wondered for a moment if we should call the police, but suddenly he recalled that he had left it down the hill at the market the night before and, lost in thought, had walked home. We laughed very hard as I realized I was married to an absent-minded professor.

During my entire pregnancy, I suffered serious morning sickness. I was prescribed drugs to help, but threw up at home and in gutters if walking outside—pretty funny in retrospect, but not at the time. My grammar school friend, Suzy, shared afternoon teatime with me and brought her adorable daughter Caroline. Suzy became pregnant with Jeffrey, so my baby was going to be sandwiched between my oldest friend's two children. Surrounded by good friends, and a kind and loving husband, it was a special time of my life. Jerry and I had fun times with friends and department colleagues. I liked Arthur Fisher, Tony Tromba, Ralph Abraham—all from UC Santa Cruz—and also Darryl Holm from New Mexico, and John Ball from England. Other local friends were Alan and Margo Weinstein.

In Berkeley with Jerry, I attended math department colloquium dinners, often at Chinese restaurants.

In the spring of 1976, when I was thirty-three, Tony arranged a photo show for me at Cowell College in a small gallery at UC Santa Cruz. I was very pregnant, but enjoyed the show and the accolades. Several weeks later when Tony visited us in Berkeley, I drove him to the hospital emergency room because of his kidney stone attack. I was nine months pregnant, and when we walked into the lobby at Herrick Hospital, the nurses took one look at me, thinking I was about to deliver, and said we should be at a different hospital. We set them straight, and Tony was taken care of immediately.

Alison was due on June 7, but I wasn't in labor yet that Tuesday, so I walked slowly to the neighborhood polling place down the street and voted for Jimmy Carter in the primary. Then on June 9, 1976, Alison was born at 10:55 a.m. at Kaiser Hospital in Oakland after a ten-hour labor. Jerry was with me throughout, coaching my breathing and feeding me lemon drops. It was not customary then, as it is today, to have ultrasound during the pregnancy, so we did not know beforehand whether the baby would be a boy or girl. We had a healthy child we named Alison Lesley Marsden. We chose the name because we liked it and I had a favorite cousin named Alison. The many flower bouquets delivered to my hospital room from friends and relatives were a wonderful surprise. I had never felt so honored.

Alison had newborn jaundice, a common occurrence, and had to be in an incubator under bilirubin lights, and I was allowed to stay there for five days. Nurses on different shifts would come in and say, "Are you still here?" I was visited by a few friends, including Mary Ellen and Frank Ackerman, who were in the area from Death Valley. Jerry was very calm and attentive despite the fact that it was the end of his academic year as vice chairman of the math department and he was under a lot of pressure. We drove Alison home from the hospital in the little blue Volkswagen station wagon to Rose Street in Berkeley where we were still renting a house.

When Alison was about two weeks old, my mother flew in from Hawaii where my parents were living by then. She was very helpful and loved seeing her new grandchild. Alison would be her second grandchild, preceded only by my brother's son Colin who was six at the time. It was very unusual for my mother to fly anywhere without my father, who had stayed behind in Hawaii, but they talked every night on the phone, and I remember her asking him what he did and what he ate each day. They were very close and dependent on each other's company. She stayed a week only, but it was a good visit. We also saw my aunt Arline Eckbo, who lived in Berkeley by then.

The next few months passed quickly, though we had many sleepless nights. When Alison was two months old, we bravely attempted a car camping trip to Tuolumne Meadows in Yosemite. We soon discovered that the most difficult part was what to do with a crying baby in the middle of the night, trapped with us in a tent. During the days, we hiked in the meadows and did a gentle climb up Pothole Dome. Jerry's eight-year old son, Christopher, had come from Canada to visit us for a few weeks. We left early because we were very tired, and Jerry said, "You know, we don't have to do this." I agreed that perhaps I didn't always have to be so rugged. On the way home, we pulled off when Chris threw up all over the gear shift and Alison was in need of a major diaper change.

I was finding out that family life wasn't going to be easy, and like many new moms, I felt that my wings had been clipped. I experienced an odd range of feelings, loving my baby, but being very tired and overwhelmed. I was nursing Alison, and sleep deprivation was new to me, but Jerry was calm throughout and had a soothing influence on me. He was good at getting up in the early morning and letting me sleep while Alison lay beside him in his study, cooing on a blanket on the floor. He was a natural at parenting—changing diapers, swaddling and rocking Alison in his arms.

In September, when Alison was three months old, I traveled alone with her to Hawaii to stay for a few weeks with my parents at their home on Oahu while Jerry was attending a conference in Europe. Being in Hawaii with a baby was very comfortable, especially with my parents there to help, but it wasn't without problems because I was having nursing issues, and I was frustrated not hearing from Jerry, who was so far away. We didn't have easy communication with cell phones and computers as we do today. However, the balmy air and breezes in Hawaii were soothing, and we were able to lay Alison out on the floor on a blanket in the outdoor lanai. We entertained ourselves watching her lift her tiny head and wiggle her hands and feet. My father carried her all over the yard, showing her each shrub, flower, and tree and telling her what they were. She had her first nature lessons with him.

He also was the one who noticed that her eyes might be crossed. As a new mother, I thought all babies had crossed eyes, and I didn't want to believe it, but he was right. Later when I returned to Berkeley, we started visiting Dr. Alan Chasnoff at the Oakland Kaiser, and he determined that she had alternating crossed eyes. Surgery wouldn't help, but little glasses and eye exercises eventually did. At that stage, we just patched one eye at a time to help strengthen the muscles in the other. We saw Dr. Chasnoff for many years and even followed him when he became the head of ophthalmology at the new Kaiser in Martinez. Alison's eye problems are not detectable today except during exams with professionals. (In 2016, I happened to read a Kaiser bulletin that said Dr. Chasnoff had just retired. By this time Alison was forty years old.)

Jerry, Alison, and I returned to Hawaii at Christmas that year in 1976 and enjoyed taking walks on the beach with Alison in a Kelty baby pack on Jerry's back. She and Jerry had matching floppy hats, and Alison had her first muumuu, a tiny pink-and-white flowered dress. Larry and his son Colin also joined us there for the holidays, and the balmy Hawaiian weather was wonderful. (Larry had married my high school friend, Francie Oman, but by this time they were divorced.) My parents' one-story, rambling house was comfortable and breezy, and they continued their interest in remodeling, but now they hired workers to improve a bathroom and add a swimming pool.

These days they no longer did all their own gardening, and I was happy to see they had a gardener who came weekly to trim hedges, mow the large lawn, and clean up coconuts. My father treasured his koi pond and protected it from toads he called by their Latin name "Bufos." I even found him out at night whacking them on the lawn with a shovel! Over the next few years, we would return there for visits as often as we could. The house sat back from a canal and was walking distance to a beach where we often swam, built sandcastles, and watched waves. Our favorite restaurant was an open-air, casual beachside place called Buzz's Steak House, which I understand is still there today and a favorite of Barack Obama's.

After returning home to Berkeley in January 1977, we sublet our rental for six months to a visiting professor and family. Then we boarded the plane for Edinburgh, Scotland, where Jerry was on sabbatical at Heriot-Watt University a few miles out of the city. Colleagues there had arranged for us to rent a remodeled cottage on an old farm where all the buildings had been turned into nice dwellings. We arrived in the middle of winter, but bottled milk was on the doorstep, and the heat was on. It was a small adorable two-story cottage with two bedrooms and a bath upstairs, and a modern kitchen, dining room, and living room down. The kitchen opened out onto a private enclosed garden with lawn surrounded by flower beds, of course not blooming at that time. By spring, I would have it completely planted and colorful; the landlord was delighted and said it had never looked so good.

For the next six months, we lived in the cottage. We bought a small car and learned to drive on the left side of the road. It was amazing to me how quickly my brain could make that change; I guess life depended on it. Jerry usually walked to work along a country lane that passed a stable. The university was not far away. Sometimes I used the car to drive into Edinburgh and go shopping and sightseeing. More often, I pushed Alison in her stroller over to a fairly new indoor mall where I could stock up on groceries. I lost weight quickly after my pregnancy and, before long, was in great shape from all the walking. In addition, I washed cloth diapers (nappies) and hung them out on the line where they usually froze that winter. The cottage was often draped with drying laundry, and I used those nappies for many years after as rags.

We had not been in Scotland for long before Jerry had to return to the States to work with Alan Weinstein on a calculus book they were writing, so I was alone with a baby for about ten days. It was hard as I knew just a few people by then, but had to manage the long days and nights mostly alone. Our cottage was in the country, but right near the railroad tracks. There was always a 2:00 a.m. train that roared by, and it was a nightly adventure for Alison to wake up and want to play. We had quite a time trying to get her on a nighttime schedule while we lived there.

We celebrated Alison's first birthday in Switzerland while on a brief trip for Jerry to give a talk in Geneva. After the talk, we traveled to a small Swiss town where we had arranged to stay in a chalet for a few days. It was a lovely chalet and surroundings, but we had ignored the calendar and arrived there during a religious holiday with no food to be found. I was still nursing Alison, so she was fine, but Jerry and I had to eat baby food out of jars until we finally found an open restaurant. Not all was lost, however, because the weather was great that June 9, 1977, and we made some beautiful hikes above the town. I remember a meaningful talk we had while hiking; Alison was on Jerry's back in the baby pack. We decided to not have any more children because we wanted to focus on raising Alison and her half brother Chris, who came to be with us each summer. We felt fulfilled with what we had, and life was good. I remember the conversation and where we were standing surrounded by beautiful Swiss mountains and sunny green slopes. In the future, we occasionally revisited our decision, but still agreed, and it felt right at the time.

In the summer after we returned to Edinburgh, Chris came alone all the way from Toronto on the plane to stay with us for a few weeks. He was nine years old at the time, but such a beautiful, brave little guy. He was always upbeat and eager to do anything we suggested. He played happily with Alison in the garden behind the house; he pushed her around in her little go cart and helped her learn to walk. Looking back now, I realize what a cheerful, kind, young boy he was. The early home movies are still fun to watch. At the time, my father had loaned me a Super 8 movie camera so I could send my parents movies of those early months of Alison's life. My parents celebrated their fortieth wedding anniversary that summer while we were far away, but I still remember combing a beach in Scotland and wanting to send them forty smooth beach pebbles. However, the pebbles are probably still there where they belong because of the cost of the postage.

Earlier that spring, I needed some free time to photograph in Edinburgh and visit museums, shops, and the beautiful Laura Ashley store. I had hired a middle-aged woman as a babysitter. Alice, who had children of her own, had posted an ad looking for work. I was nervous at first to leave my baby with a stranger, but Alice became part of the family, and we part of hers. She usually came to the cottage to take care of Alison, but eventually asked if she could occasionally push her in her stroller to her mother's cottage nearby. I was glad I consented, because her mother was a dear old woman. I sometimes went there for afternoon tea, and for many years later, I corresponded with her at Christmastime. Sadly, a few years later when Jerry, Alison, and I returned to Edinburgh for a short visit, we discovered that Alice had died of cancer. Her mother, husband, and children had outlived her.

While living in Scotland, Jerry and I had several opportunities to travel. Even with Alison, we managed to travel to the Isle of Skye, the Lake District in England, and many other historical places. It was hard traveling in England and Scotland with a baby because often restaurants did not have high chairs, and hotels had thin walls, but we did it anyway. I also took a lot of black-and-white photographs that I am glad to have today. One of my favorites is of two trees touching limbs in the Lake District. It was in the Lake District also that Alison said her first word, "Duck," when pointing at the ducks in Lake Windermere near Kendal. A few years later, when Alison was four, we revisited the Lake District and saw Hilltop Farm, the home of Beatrix Potter who wrote the Peter Rabbit books. We had a delightful cottage tour, which was perfect for our young tourist Alison.

When Chris visited us in Scotland in the summer of 1977, we took a trip north to Loch Ness (no monster seen) and on to stay in our landlord's croft, which was up on the windswept west coast. We were to pick up our milk from the neighbors who invited us into their smoke-filled, poorly lit home. They were unlike anyone I had ever met. Their Scots brogue was so strong we could hardly understand them. To them, we were probably like aliens from outer space, but they seemed to enjoy our visit and loved seeing the children. I photographed them outside their croft, and I'm happy they were willing to pose for me and that I had the nerve to ask.

On weekends near our Edinburgh cottage, we did spring hiking in the Pentland Hills, up and over stiles and through sheep pastures. There were many new lambs. One day, when hiking with another family, Alison tried to eat sheep poop when we placed her on the ground. Our friend's older kids were howling with excitement. We often had British colleagues of Jerry's visit, and they enjoyed outings with us, either hiking or visiting Edinburgh Castle. Most memorable to me were John Ball, David and Vicki Rand, and Ruth and Phil Holmes. Alison still knows some of them today. Ruth and Phil hosted us in Princeton many years later when Alison was beginning college there. In the summer of 2017, Alison revisited Edinburgh Castle with her family and has a photo of herself with her two children at the same exact spot where a photo was taken of her on Jerry's back in 1977.

In July, that summer of 1977, we flew home via Toronto, Canada, to drop Chris off with his mother at the airport. We visited Jerry's mother, Isobel—known to all her grandchildren as "Drama" because one of her young grandchildren couldn't pronounce Gramma. After our visit, Jerry left from there go to a conference, and I flew to International Falls, Minnesota, to visit my National Park Service friends the Ackermans, whom I had known in Death Valley. Now, we all had small children and went canoeing at Voyageurs National Park in the Boundary Waters Canoe Area where Frank was now stationed. At their home in town, Mary Ellen had a wonderful vegetable garden that surpassed the one she tried to develop in Death Valley where she and I had hauled wild burro manure off the road for her compost pile. Since our visit at Voyageurs, we have only met a couple of times, but we still exchange Christmas cards these forty years later.

When Jerry and I returned to Berkeley the summer of 1977, we continued living on Rose Street for a few months, but our friends' house at 1602 Marin Avenue, Albany, came up for sale. I had lived in the rental apartment in the basement previously, so we knew it would be a good way for us to start out. We bought it directly from the owners for $66,000 and moved in when Alison was about eighteen months old. The main floor had two bedrooms and one bath plus an attic area where Jerry could have his home office. I was able to make a darkroom in the laundry room downstairs off the garage. For several years we rented out the basement apartment, our most memorable tenant being Channing Ahn, a delightful Cal student who made wonderful banana bread. I still have his recipe today. We also rented to Linda Yemoto, who was a naturalist at the Tilden Park Little Farm and Nature Area, a place we often frequented with Alison when she was very small.

After moving into our new home, I met Lubov and Mike Mazur over the back fence. We became well acquainted when they wanted to enlarge their basement by digging it out. Lubov and I decided to use the dirt to make a vegetable garden on the property line. Alison loved playing in the dirt and one day had her "first urm scare" when she discovered earthworms. Lubov and Mike became close friends, and we were also close to Lubov's parents. Lubov's mother, Vera, was Ukrainian and a young athlete during World War II. Her athletic career as an Olympian shotput contestant was denied because of the war, and she ended up in Germany. There she met Lubov's dad, Bill, who was a GI. They became attracted to each other in a basketball game and dated, even though neither spoke the other's native language. They married and came to the United States after the war and settled in the Bay Area. One spring ritual for us was going to their house in Walnut Creek, where Vera would pick fresh scallions from her abundant garden and make us sandwiches with scallions and pork fat. The first bite was always heaven, followed by gagging and much laughter!

Lubov and Mike were upbeat, creative neighbors with whom we shared home-improvement projects and many informal dinners. They always considered Alison their "practice child" and often babysat for us. Alison loved going to Lubov and Mike's house where they always made her feel loved and included. They were clay artists who sold ceramic pins at Bay Area museums and studios, and they gave Alison her own clay drawer in the studio where she had her own tools for playing with clay. Today, it is still labeled with her name, forty years later.

For the first five years of Alison's life, I did not work outside the home. I loved my time at home and embraced the experience of watching her grow while I included activities that enriched me as well—photography and gardening. I grew flowers and vegetables, baked bread, and had a good social life. I continued my walking and hiking. One time I joined a Sierra Club hike in the Berkeley hills and made a good friend, Cynthia Schneider, a writer and friend I kept for many years. These were meaningful years for me, raising a young child and sharing time with other mothers and their young children. I joined a babysitting co-op, and we took turns caring for each other's children. By having a permanent arrangement with another couple, Jerry and I were able to go out every other Friday night. Jerry was often the one who went to their house to sit because he was happy to work quietly on his research after their baby was asleep. Sometimes the other father would sit for Alison at our house. It was nice to see men beginning to be more involved in child-rearing than when I was a child. During this period, I also continued my photography by working in my darkroom when Alison was napping. As time went on, I joined a couple of photo groups in which I could show my work. Additionally, Jerry was always very supportive of my photography, agreeing I should have time to work in my darkroom. He, himself, needed quiet research time and understood my need for the same.

About the time Alison was two, we bought a new green-and-white Volkswagen bus. This was my second bus, but not to be my last. It was a partial camper with fold-down bed, table, and closet. We traveled a lot to Owens Valley, Death Valley, and the Southwest. One time, we visited my high school friend, Nancy Piver, who had married into a ranching family in San Luis Obispo, and she gave us a bumper sticker from the Mozart Festival that read, "Even cowboys need Mozart." Afterward, in New Mexico, we were nearly run off the road by a pickup truck, so we reluctantly decided to remove the sticker. We realized that VW buses with bumper stickers could be a freethinking symbol even in the '70s. When we camped in the bus, Alison was small enough to sleep on a cozy bed we'd made for her on the floor while we stretched out in comfort above.

One fall season, my friend Wendy Niles, Alison, and I took a girls' road trip to Capitol Reef National Park in Utah. I really felt like a free spirit during this trip—back on the road with beautiful fall colors and visiting national parks that had become such an important part of my life. Alison was a good traveler, and Wendy and I took turns driving and entertaining her while she was secure in her car seat. We camped at Zion and Capitol Reef for a few days where I took a lot of black-and-white photographs with a new Hasselblad camera. Wendy also took photos and collected natural materials for her weavings. We met other campers who joined us for hikes and meals around the campfire in one of my all-time favorite campgrounds nestled in an old orchard at Capitol Reef National Monument. Since then, I've returned to it many times.

During the summer, when Alison was two, Jerry and I made arrangements to rent burros in the eastern Sierra at Pine Creek Pack Station, and we made a hiking trip to Honeymoon Lake with our friends Lubov and Mike. Jerry carried Alison on his back in the kid pack, and the rest of us were in charge of leading the loaded burros up the steep trail. Their names were Tommy and Mozzo, and the packer had said they would "go better in pairs," and that "they loved cigarettes," which we didn't have. He taught us how to load up our gear and waved us goodbye. We were on our own.

It was quite a climb to the lake and took most of the day up from the pack station. The altitude was difficult, Lubov got very sick, but Alison did great and loved toddling around the campsite in her tiny hiking boots. In camp, we hobbled the burros and they grazed nearby where we could hear the bell around Tommy's neck. We were well prepared with warm clothes and a cute little kid's red down sleeping bag. However, when it started to snow, we all decided we'd better break camp, so we packed up the burros with all our gear and made a hasty descent back to the pack station. Boy, were the packers glad to see us, saying they were worried about our little girl camping in the snow! We waved goodbye to Tommy and Mozzo and headed back down to lower elevation and a warm motel in Owens Valley.

During the summer of 1979, when Alison was three and Chris was ten, we often traveled to the Sierra for camping trips. By this time, things were more manageable with the kids, and we had fun scouting around and camping with the VW bus and a tent. One time, we went north of Truckee to Lakes Basin Recreation Area where I had been as a teenager with my family. In the campground, we awoke one morning, and Alison's eyes were nearly swollen shut, probably from an allergic reaction to an insect or spider bite. We broke camp and drove an hour south to the Truckee hospital emergency room where they gave her an antihistamine shot and blew up surgical gloves like balloons to entertain her. All was well, and we returned home safely.

That summer, we had also been searching for a ski cabin to purchase with our friends Julie Donnelly, her husband, Mike Nolan, and David Goldschmidt, our friend from the math department. We considered areas around Truckee and Donner Lake and eventually settled on a modest, affordable ($65,000) two-bedroom cabin at a development called Tahoe-Donner. We purchased it late summer and quickly furnished and prepared it for winter. Our friends started using it then, but we didn't until January because Jerry, Alison, and I took off for three months in Canada.

Jerry had sabbatical again, and we went to Calgary, Alberta, for three months at the University of Calgary. While there, we enrolled Alison in a day care class where she could meet other children, and I joined a hiking/ skiing group that went to Banff National Park almost weekly. This was a wonderful, group of rugged women; the leader was a cancer survivor, who was sixty-five at the time. I was thirty-six by this time, and I began to see myself as a conditioned hiker/skier again. On weekends, Jerry and I would always take Alison somewhere with us on an outdoor excursion, often to Banff or Kananaskis Valley which were an hour or two away.

One time, camping in Banff, we slept in a tent close to our VW bus, thinking Alison was safely tucked away inside the bus. In the early morning light, we heard a rustling sound and looked out of our tent to see a large bear on its hind feet looking into the bus windows on the passenger side. We scared it away by clanging pots and pans, but when we arose, we discovered that Jerry had left the driver's window open all night. There were paw prints on both sides of the bus. Yes, I was married to an absent-minded professor, but luckily, Alison was safe.

It was at the Banff Library where we had tea after hikes on the weekends, and they gave Alison "pussycat tea," mostly milk—and, thereafter, a family tradition. I still serve pussycat tea to my grandchildren today. We also drove the Icefields Parkway where the glaciers came right down near the road. We did short hikes and enjoyed the spectacular fall colors, notably the yellow aspen and larch trees. Sometimes we hiked together, but often with colleagues or visiting friends.

One time my friend Cindy Schneider from Berkeley came to visit, and while Jerry cared for Alison, she and I took a three-day trip in the cold weather. We were the last guests one night at Numtijah Lodge, an old historical place next to a beautiful lake near the Icefield Parkway. We had the place to ourselves, and on the next day, we hiked on a long open snowy trail where we spotted two moose. We knew to keep our distance, as moose can be very dangerous, and watched as they lumbered down the slope to the river below.

In Calgary, Jerry and I socialized with several couples, sometimes hiking or skiing, sometimes over dinner. The Sniatycki family took us up the hill behind their house to ride their horses in a huge area of open grassland that overlooked the city. Soon the weather was freezing every night, and we had to have an engine heater installed on our VW so we could plug it in each night outside the apartment complex. In Calgary, this is called "plug-in weather" on the news. One time, I drove the bus across town to visit friends, but by the time I left their house, I could barely get the engine to start. For years later, back in California, our bus had a small cord hanging out of the engine compartment, and only those in the know could recognize what it was.

While we were in Canada, the Sniatyckis introduced us to their Siberian husky. We ended up buying one of our own—Atu, a six-month-old husky—from an older couple who decided they couldn't handle him. We should have listened to them, as we observed this huge six-month-old puppy jumping all over their furniture. I was intrigued with the idea of having a sled dog, and we soon took him out to Lake Louise, which was frozen solid by then. There were people all over the lake—walking, skating, and skiing across the beautiful lake surrounded by tall, dramatic mountains. We hooked Atu up to our friends' dogsled and put three-year-old Alison in the seat. Almost immediately, we ended up at a full chase when Atu took off across the lake with Alison. Atu was born to pull, but training was clearly needed. What were we thinking?

Before Christmas, when it came time to return home from Calgary, Jerry flew home with Alison while I enjoyed the adventure of driving the VW home with one of Jerry's colleagues and Atu the dog. I loved the wide-open spaces that time of year with few crowds and cozy cafés; at one in Dubois, Idaho, I pronounced the name in French and was quickly corrected with *Dew*boyz. Atu was a good traveler, but we should have left him in the cold climate of Canada; I spent the next several years vacuuming dog hair and locking gates. He had a strong instinct for hunting down the neighbors' cats and bringing them home as souvenirs to drop by his doghouse. For the cats that did survive, we paid some expensive vet bills, and we finally decided that we had to give him away to a single man with a big fence. We were heartbroken, but we had to admit that buying him had been a mistake.

Back at home in Albany, we enrolled Alison at Skytown Nursery School up in the hills in Kensington. We had reserved a spot before going to Calgary; now she was three and a half years old and ready for school. As soon as we arrived, we met Kara Flanigon and her mother and father, Mary Jo Cittadino and Mike Flanigon, who said they had heard about us and had been waiting for us to return. We all lived in Albany and could share driving, friendship, and babysitting. Eventually, the girls were like sisters, and we were able to leave Alison with the Flanigons occasionally when we traveled. My first long trip away from her was to Los Alamos, New Mexico, with Jerry, and I really felt awful until I called and was assured by Mike that Alison was doing well.

Alison and Kara developed a friendship that lasted all through elementary school and thereafter. They played together often and sometimes got into mischief. One time, they spread Johnson's baby powder all over Alison's new dark blue, wall-to-wall carpet and her furniture and toys as well. After that, I paid a little more attention to what was going on behind closed doors, but usually just heard the delightful sound of imaginative play. When it came time to start kindergarten, we enrolled them in the afternoon class so we could continue to enjoy leisurely mornings for one more year before first grade. School was within walking distance. The crossing guard, Pearl, adored Alison and gave her a handmade Christmas tree ornament that we still hang on the tree today.

As the years passed, Alison was invited on trips with the Flanigons to visit their relatives in Los Angeles and to see Disneyworld in Florida. In recent years, when Alison traveled east, she visited Mike and Mary Jo where they lived in Washington, DC, and also attended Kara's wedding in Pennsylvania.

After I enrolled Alison in nursery school, I started a docent volunteer training program at Audubon Canyon Ranch at Bolinas Lagoon, north of San Francisco. The ocean breezes and fog roll in over the canyon, which is a wooded, serene refuge set aside to protect the nesting habitat of great blue herons and American egrets. My training classes occurred one day a week for eighteen weeks during the fall/winter of 1979. Bolinas Lagoon was over an hour's drive from the East Bay, but I carpooled with two other women, both in their midsixties and good role models for my future. The training program was very thorough, teaching us about the nesting habits of herons and egrets, as well as identifying shore birds and learning about pond life. It was a wonderful way for me to connect with the out-of-doors as I had in the national parks. In addition to the training program, the group of women had many interesting outings for nature study and bird watching, and I was completely in my element. We went north on overnight trips to Grey Lodge Wildlife Refuge near Marysville to see the migrating ducks, sand hill cranes, and snow geese that landed in that area on a spectacular yearly migration. We boated on the glassy, serene waters of Bolinas Lagoon which was fed by tidal currents, and we hiked in Sonoma Country in the coastal habitat of madrone, bay, oak, and redwood trees. For three years I gained experience at leading nature walks for children and adults, and this would eventually lead me into elementary school teaching, though I didn't know it at the time.

When Alison was young, Jerry and I enrolled her in many classes up the hill at the Lawrence Hall of Science above UC Berkeley. She pronounced it "the Lower Hall of Science." Of course, we could not know that she would end up getting married there someday. Alison and her friend Kara took a class called "Math for Girls" which was aimed at preventing the math anxiety that many girls of earlier generations had developed. At home with Alison, Jerry made simple illustrated math books showing "one piece of toast plus one piece of toast, equal two pieces of toast." We still have the little books, and I am sure Jerry's creative help encouraged her to develop a positive attitude toward mathematics and science that has stayed with her to this day. We felt it was very important at the time, and both she and her husband are now passing on the importance of a well-rounded education to their children.

When Alison was young, I attended a two-week Oliver Gagliani photo workshop in Virginia City, Nevada. Oliver was a renowned San Francisco photographer who mastered the art of the black-and-white print. This was my first workshop away from home, but by this time, Alison was in first grade, and Jerry took good care of her while I was away. I also taught beginning and intermediate photography part-time at the student union on the Berkeley campus. These experiences were good, but I began to look ahead to what I might do for a career outside of photography. I was becoming frustrated trying to become a showing/recognized artist, and college teaching positions were hard to find. Becoming an elementary school teacher, with a slant on environmental studies, seemed a good fit for my life. I could share school holidays with Alison and Jerry and have summers free for photography and travel. Most of my photography friends held mainstream jobs and did photography on the side. I started taking classes at Cal State Hayward to work toward a teaching credential.

After completing my credential when Alison was in second grade, the principal at her school suggested that I apply for a job. Unfortunately, just before I was interviewed in August 1984, my father had emergency open-heart surgery, and I was very uneasy during the interview. They did not hire me for the kindergarten job I wanted, but I was hired for a six-month substitute job teaching first grade. That was a tough time for me—teaching six-year-olds during the day and driving to St. Mary's Hospital in San Francisco each evening to visit my dad, who was intubated due to pneumonia. Six weeks after school started, he died from complications at the young age of seventy.

It was one of the worst periods of my life because I had to divide myself between work, where first graders tugged on my skirt, and family, where my mother and brother needed my emotional strength. Before my dad died, I have a distinct memory of Alison in the waiting room at the hospital, gluing together a small wooden sailboat with Popsicle sticks that she labeled the *Saint Mary*. Perhaps it was a symbolic lifeboat for her grandpa; we still have it today. I didn't think of it at the time, but looking back, I see I could have used a lifeboat myself. It was a tough time.

As time passed, life continued with the familiarity of house projects and socializing with Lubov and Mike over impromptu evening meals. They developed an enthusiasm for installing wood-burning stoves in their home. We put one in ours also, and the four of us went wood gathering wherever we could find free scrap wood in our urban area. One time we made the mistake of gathering driftwood on the waterfront at low tide, not thinking of the creosote smoke that would result when it was burned. So much for free wood! Just the same, it was fun to look at woodstoves at the Whole Earth Catalog Store on Telegraph Avenue in Berkeley. It was there that Lubov and I bought our Kitchen Aid mixers and launched into making bread and other delicious foods. We visited the Monterey Market for our produce, made good coffee and tea, and ate well. Our lives were intertwined in a casual, humorous, and over-the-fence way.

Jerry continued teaching at Berkeley during those years. Before I started teaching full-time, we traveled and stayed in Europe. When Alison was about to turn four, Jerry had sabbatical, and we went to England to the University of Warwick for four months. While there, we lived on campus in modern housing for visiting faculty. Our cottage had a study with a curved blackboard. We enrolled Alison in a preschool across the campus where we could walk back and forth. Also, we bought a car and drove to nearby areas like Kenilworth and Stratford-upon-Avon. We were friends with David and Vicki Rand and often visited their home in Kenilworth.

Vicki and I loved to sew and visited the Laura Ashley store in Birmingham once to buy enough fabric to make bedspreads. Our kids played together in the Kenilworth Common and their backyard garden.

By this time Alison was wearing a little red wool coat that I bought in Stratford. On her fourth birthday, we were visiting Warwick Castle, and she was wearing a paper crown, made at the preschool, which told everyone that it was her birthday. That day we rowed on the river, went to a park where she rode a little train, and visited the famous castle up on the hill overlooking the river. Later in the day, we visited a colleague's home in Warwick where we met Stephen Hawking with his wife, Jane, and the two children they had at the time. All the kids played together outside. I was shyly impressed with the Hawkings, and I didn't want to stare at Stephen in a wheelchair assisted by Jane. It was 1980, and he lived until 2018 when I was writing this memoir.

On future trips, Jerry, Alison, and I visited France, Germany, northern England, Scotland again, and Iceland. After Alison started school, these trips were in the summers, though on the trip to Iceland we took her out of school and celebrated her ninth birthday in Rekjavik with Jerry's Icelandic graduate student Bjorn Birnir and his wife, Inga. We swam in the Blue Lagoon, a huge public swimming pool with natural thermally heated water and hot tubs along the side. They also toured us around some nearby sites. Notable was a hike to a flowing hot spring where we went swimming on a very cold, cloudy day. I remember stepping from lichen-covered hummock to hummock. It was a very unique, treeless landscape and easy to see the beautiful landforms.

In addition, while we were staying there in student housing, we were able to hear and view, from a distance, the first landing of the Concorde jet from France. I was also impressed that Iceland had a woman president. En route to Iceland, we had stopped for a few days in Washington, DC, where Jerry had a conference. While he was busy, Alison and I went to the Smithsonian Museums. She did this with such adult interest and stamina, I was impressed, and as I tired, I sat down on a bench at the Museum of Art while she looked at every painting in the room. Her second-grade teacher had shown the kids reproductions by famous artists, and Alison was able to recognize their styles firsthand.

Alison was about eight or nine when she joined the Junior Ranger program in Tilden Park in the Berkeley hills. From the time, she was a baby, we had made weekend outings to the Little Farm and the Tilden Merry-Go-Round as well as the little train. Now, she was old enough to be in the Saturday morning program led by Ranger Tim. They hiked, kissed banana slugs, learned one hundred ways to use a bandana, and built native shelters out of branches and bark. Once a month, they backpacked overnight, rain or shine, and sang continuously. They also took longer summer overnight trips to Big Sur, Yosemite, and East Bay Regional Parks. Alison loved Junior Rangers and the outdoor life, and we loved having her experience that.

During the years of Alison's early childhood, Jerry and I were very happy together. I loved my role as a mom, enjoyed meeting others with children, and had a good balance of parenting as well as my own self-expression through piano lessons and photography. When Alison was in third grade, we decided to move to North Berkeley to a bigger Tudor style house in a quieter neighborhood. It was sad to move away from our good neighbors, but we were still close and visited often. At the new house on Vincente Avenue, I had a larger, more complete darkroom built by our friend Zander Brennan, who was beginning his career as a contractor. My basement darkroom was one of his early jobs. We also had him remodel our kitchen, which turned out beautifully with earth-tone tiles, oak floors, and ceiling.

Jerry continued to travel to conferences, I was teaching, and Chris came to live with us full-time to complete high school. Jerry traveled a lot, and when he was gone, I discovered that Chris was climbing out his bedroom window at night to smoke. I was often left in charge of it all—shopping, cooking, helping with both kids' homework, driving, plus my own job. Our lives had become much more stressful as we had become a two-career household.

We struggled along, went to counseling, but within a couple of years, when Alison was in fifth grade, and Chris a senior, Jerry and I decided to separate. For some time, we had been growing apart, and I suspected he had a wandering eye. It seemed the marriage could not withstand outside influences. He wanted more time for work and travel to conferences, and I wanted more time with like-minded or artistic friends. I couldn't appreciate then, as I do today, how important it was for Jerry to have time to himself at home for research. It always felt like he was escaping from me and family matters, though he seemed to always find time for his colleagues. In hindsight, I know that Jerry had a tough time growing up, due to his father's drinking and mental health, and he told me that he used to close himself in his room to study math, even plugging his ears to avoid the arguments between his parents.

In our home, his research was also his refuge. At Berkeley, his job was very demanding, and mathematics was a lonely business for me; I would prepare dinner parties for his colleagues, but then I couldn't understand a word of what was being discussed at the table. Our counselling was often interrupted by his travels, and we both arrived at the conclusion that it was time to part. Eventually, we split up and divorced in 1988. We were so decent with each other we were able to use the same lawyer and work out details. I kept the house (and the mortgage), and Jerry kept his royalties and retirement. It seemed a fair settlement and helped us get through the tough period. Jerry moved to an apartment in Emeryville with Chris, and I had custody of Alison, though she spent some weekends and trips with Jerry. That first summer they went to China together. It felt pretty weird at the airport to be dropping her off and not getting on the plane with them. She had a good trip where she was sometimes watched by graduate students while Jerry lectured, and she even bicycled through Tiananmen Square. She ate a lot of new foods and reported being a little homesick on a Yangtze River cruise. I still have some small cloisonné boxes they brought back to me, one with a cute cricket design because Alison and I had been reading *The Cricket in Times Square* at school.

It has always been a source of regret for me that Jerry and I couldn't work things out, especially for Alison's and Chris's sakes. Sadly, I was told that Chris thought it was his fault that we split up, but that wasn't true. Jerry and I did the best we could by not bad-mouthing each other over the years and not dragging the kids through our adult problems. We were decent and friendly for years after, though we did not see each other very much as the years went on. I eventually lost touch with Chris and have seen him just a couple of times since, but Alison still sees him from time to time. He became a truck driver on cross-country hauls and has a driving partner who is also his fiancé. He sends good road stories to Alison online.

A few years later Jerry married a German woman several years younger, and they moved to Pasadena, where Jerry took a prestigious job at Cal Tech. Unfortunately, this was a tough time for Alison and, I think, also for Jerry, who buried himself further in his research and teaching. Sadly, Jerry developed prostate cancer in his fifties and spent many years battling the disease until his death in September 2010 at age sixty-eight. He was a beloved professor, author, and researcher and has been sorely missed by many students and colleagues throughout the world, as well as his family. It makes me sad to think of his early death.

Alison and her family are still connected to her Canadian relatives who live in the Vancouver, BC, area—her aunt Judy, cousins Cindy, Judy Jr., and cousin Teresa who lives in Nova Scotia. They still visit together in Gibsons, BC, on the Sunshine Coast.

On August 18, 2017, when Alison was forty-one, she wrote this about her dad:

> Yesterday would have been my father's seventy-fifth birthday. I'm thankful for my memories of him and for the example he set for me and all those he touched: his love of science and collaboration, his thoughtful and loving manner, the kind and gentle way he interacted with others, and his quiet curiosity about the world around him.

We will all remember Jerry as a soft-spoken, gentle, and generous man, with a soft sense of humor. When Alison was young, he would say things like "Daddy do it!" when helping her out, or "Ope it" instead of open your mouth when he was feeding her. Then there were lots of "Bobby the Frog" stories that he made up for both kids. Comments for adults included "We're grown-ups; we can do what we want!" And when driving the car and getting cut off by some bad driver, he would calmly say, "Thanks, George!" Recently, I remembered that he and I used to say, "ET, phone home!" when parting. One time when he was on an extension ladder repairing the bay windows, the ladder slipped, he fell into the juniper bushes, came into the house, sat down, and said, "I am an academic, and I can't do this stuff anymore." There was a lot of humor with our neighbors, and many "Daddy blew it!" stories, which were all in jest, with him laughing as hard as the rest of us. We still say it today in his memory.

Jerry Marsden, 1976

Jerry at Bay to Breakers Race in San Francisco, 1976

Grandma Ferne with Alison 1976

Alison and Nancy, 1977

Chris at Loch Ness, Scotland, summer 1977

Jerry and Alison, Briones Park nature lesson

Alison and Grandpa Ed

Alison on wood-cutting day, Truckee

Alison and Kara Flanigon playing dress-up

Jerry, Alison, and Chris camping at East Lake, California

Alison camping

Alison, age seven (portrait by author)

CHAPTER 4

From Hiking Boots to Horseshoes

When Jerry and I parted, Alison and I stayed in the family home in north Berkeley for about a year until we moved to a small hillside home at 175 Val Vista Avenue in Mill Valley. It needed interior remodeling, but it had a private, picturesque setting in the canyon above the golf course. We couldn't see the course, but we could hear people shouting, "Fore!" which meant "Watch out!" when balls went astray.

We settled in before the remodeling was finished; the first stage was new windows, some new walls, a sliding door to the deck, and a new closet for the room Alison adopted downstairs. The kitchen remodel would come later. I did a lot of painting and felt as if I was carrying on my parents' tradition of working on house projects. Outside, I loved the aroma of bay laurel and coastal redwood trees again. It felt great to be back in Mill Valley because it felt like home. We had friendly neighbors including one family, the Herrmanns; Christy Herrmann taught kindergarten at Strawberry School where I was soon hired to teach fourth/fifth grade. I was chosen for the job by the principal Judy Cooper, who had been nudged by an old friend, Ralph Brott, who was now the principal of Mill Valley Middle School. My experience helped, as did the fact that I had grown up in Mill Valley. I had attended Strawberry School as a child, so returning there to teach was a pinch-myself moment. I still remember mustering up my courage as I walked into the school for Meet the Teacher Night. Judy Cooper was a warm and encouraging principal and also had a wonderful sense of humor as shown by her private comment that night calling it "Meet the Creature Night." She also told me later that I had the parents in the palm of my hand when she peeked into my classroom.

Alison and I adjusted gradually to living in Mill Valley. I dated my delightful friend George Cagwin, who bounced up the trail as we made weekly climbs of Mount Tamalpais. George and I were both divorced, and we resumed an old friendship with hiking, folk dancing, singing, and barbecues on his deck with its San Francisco view. My relationship with George ultimately did not work out for me—melding two families and schedules—but we have remained lifelong friends. We eventually both remarried and still gather with old friends in Mill Valley or at local beaches for picnics. George always rallies our old gang back together.

Alison had success with her studies and won a scholarship for private clarinet lessons, but it took most of the year for her to make good friends. On Saturdays, I drove her back to Berkeley so she could continue her participation in the Junior Ranger program in Tilden Park. I have never seen another program as good, and it was so important for Alison to continue, Jerry helped with the cross-bay travel as well.

I was engulfed in my teaching and parenting, but I wove in some photography as often as I could. I balanced a lot of things during that time, as most single parents do, but I also had a lot of fun. During the summer of 1989, I got a teacher's grant with University Research Expeditions Program (UREP) at Berkeley to go on a two-week trip to Chaco Canyon National Park, New Mexico. Our group was studying ancient Anasazi irrigation systems, and I took many black-and-white photos that were eventually used in their catalog. I had a wonderful time camping and hiking with the group, and I recall feeling, again, that I was in my element. Then, later that fall back in Mill Valley, another good thing happened; I became acquainted with Roger Brown.

Roger and I had met much earlier that year on New Year's Day at Stinson Beach in Marin County. I was there with Alison and friends playing Frisbee, and Roger was having a picnic on the beach with Deb and Scott Mills. We literally crossed paths, and after visiting with the group at the beach, we all went for a barbecue at my house in Mill Valley. I was attracted by Roger's outgoing and friendly personality and his sense of adventure. He had traveled a lot in mountains and deserts, as well as abroad. In addition, I liked the way he interacted with Alison by engaging her in conversation. Our paths had crossed once before when Deb and Scott Mills got married in 1967, and I was still married to Debbie's brother Wes. I was her matron of honor, and Roger, and his wife, Anna, had driven the getaway car. We must have been introduced then, as home movies and photos show, but in later years, we hardly remembered meeting.

When we met up again, I knew Roger was divorced, and I had heard his name mentioned by Deb and Scott over the years because he was Scott's oldest friend; they had grown up in the same neighborhood in Mill Valley. They had also spent many summers together at Lakes Basin Recreation Area in the mountains. Scott's mother, Katie Mills, had been like a second mom to Roger and had even babysat for him before Scott was born. Roger's parents had divorced when he was eight, and his mom had moved out. After that, the Mills were even more important in Roger's life. Deb and Scott were my former in-laws, and it was really nice to socialize with them again. After meeting Roger on the beach, I didn't see him again until almost a year later when I called him. He was surprised, but I knew if we didn't hit it off on the phone, there would be nothing lost. We shared several phone calls before his visit to my house, and it was easy to see that we had a lot in common; we both grew up in Mill Valley, attended Tamalpais High School, and enjoyed the out-of-doors. Since then, we have shared a wonderful home, family life, and many adventures. These days, he still thanks me for phoning him, and I am glad I did.

When I drove up to Roger's country home in Livermore for my first visit in the winter of 1990, he was picking up the mail, down at the road, and looking very tall and handsome in his work clothes and floppy ranch hat. The Victorian house beyond him on the hill was surrounded by white picket fences and seven acres of pasture. I knew he had moved and restored this old 1873 house, but it was impressive to finally see. I was to later learn that, in addition to the restoration, he had actually cut all four hundred fence pickets himself. Growing up as I had, I felt right at home with these projects. On that first visit, Roger said he wasn't sure if I would like it there because of the isolation. Little did he know. I liked him and the area and we quickly discovered how much we had in common.

Roger and I were married on the front porch of his unique home at 11450 Tesla Road, Livermore, on June 30, 1990. We had only dated each other for six months and now agree we were crazy to marry that quickly, especially since we had each been married twice before. However, we must have learned something along the way because at this writing it's been twenty-nine years, and the adventure continues.

At our wedding, we had many friends and family gather on the large wrap-around porch for the ceremony performed by our friend Michael Flanigon. Alison was fourteen, Roger's daughter Valerie was twenty-five, and his son Cameron was twenty-seven. I was forty-seven and Roger fifty-three. Both of Roger's divorced parents, Ernie and Nancy, were there, as well as my mother Ferne, Roger's brother Dennis, Dennis's fiancé Donna (who prepared all the beautiful food as a gift to us), my brother Larry, my nephew Colin, as well as many good friends and colleagues from as far away as England.

A few days after our wedding, we took off for a monthlong trip to Alaska in my blue VW Vanagon. By this time, traveling in a VW van was a lifestyle for me; I had survived a lot of miles in the flat-nosed, balky vehicles, slowly chugging uphill, but you could sleep in them, and they could go almost anywhere. We had a reservation for the van on the ferry (known as the Alaska Marine Highway) in Bellingham, Washington. There were only a few staterooms reserved months ahead, so people put up tents on the decks or slept on the floors and in recliners. You were not allowed to sleep in your car parked below and could only go there two or three times a day to walk your dog or get supplies. Had we known, we might have brought a freestanding tent for the deck, but we did know to lug our sleeping bags upstairs and quickly grab recliners or a chaise lounges inside.

One night, sandwiched in my sleeping bag on the floor between a snoring lady and Roger, I thought, *This is my honeymoon? Ah well, I am happy to be here with this handsome guy!* There was a great dining room, good company at the tables, and nice showers. We even met one friendly couple at dinner who allowed us to use the private shower in their stateroom. We disembarked with the van in Ketchikan, Juneau, and, finally, Haines, each time for a day or two. In Ketchikan, we camped in a pouring rainstorm and slept like logs with rain pounding on the roof of the van. The next morning, we discovered the Roller Bay Café on the waterfront where we enjoyed mugs of coffee and pancakes while we looked out at the moored fishing boats. We enjoyed the totem pole park, the Sitka spruce and lush vegetation. We also took a charter flight to mountainous Misty Fiords where the pilot landed on a remote lake so we could climb out on the pontoons and "fish" when he handed us a fishing pole.

After a couple of days in Ketchikan, we got back on the ferry and headed north. This time we were in "luxury" because we snagged chaise lounges on the deck, only to discover that the diesel fumes were eddying around us. When we finally disembarked at Haines, we started our drive north, but not before staying in a nice B&B and wandering around the town. This was July, so the sunsets were very late, and it never got dark at night. After enjoying our stay at the B&B, we hopped back in the VW and headed north on the Alcan Highway. At home we had worried that grocery stores would be few and far between, so we had stocked up at Costco on lots of nonperishable food, including a gigantic bag of tortilla chips that ended up coming home with us. When we finally arrived in Anchorage, we kicked ourselves as we noticed a huge Costco. We had been walking on top of canned food and maneuvering around the tortilla chips for two weeks already.

From Anchorage, we headed south to Seward to spend a few days. It was a beautiful drive passing the huge Portage Glacier and wetlands. At Seward, we camped near the bay and took a boat trip to Kenai Fjords to view glaciers, birds, seals, and whales. Back on shore, the fishermen were coming in with huge halibut and hanging them up for photos—the biggest halibut I have ever seen, some five to six feet tall and two to three hundred pounds. During the summers, many part-time workers come to Seward to work in the fish-processing plants. One fortyish gal asked if she could sleep in our campsite, and we awoke the next morning to see her out of the rain sleeping under the picnic table because she had no tent. Perhaps her trip to the bar the night before had helped. What a tough way to live in

Southeast Alaska. She had stories to tell that quickly became boring after the original novelty wore off.

We left Seward for the Kenai Peninsula, where we had sunnier weather. We had a luncheon visit with my former Death Valley friend, Sharon Gerhardt, who was in the process of a divorce from her park service husband Bob. Then Roger and I traveled as far north as Fairbanks where we stayed in another B&B in the dense woods beside a river and, to our amazement, discovered the guestbook had signatures of our good friends Judy and Stan Cooper from Mill Valley, who had beat us there by a week. We had known they were travelling in Alaska too, but we didn't know their itinerary and never saw them until we were home again in Mill Valley.

Roger and I discovered a mutual addiction on this trip—doughnuts. Every time we could, which wasn't often, we would stop for coffee and pastries and soak up the local culture. In one poorly manned café, Roger served everyone coffee like a pro; in another, we waited for service but soon realized we were supposed to help ourselves using the cups hanging on the wall. Motels were scarce, and we were lucky to have our own traveling van with bed. One rare time, we opted for a motel, walked in, and paid before looking at the room. When we discovered the room was in a modular trailer with wobbly floorboards and very grimy, I asked the motel receptionist for our money back, saying we had decided not to stay. She immediately refunded by credit card, saying, "I wouldn't want to stay here either!"

We visited Denali National Park, camping at the last campground along the paved road, and had such good weather we took the all-day shuttle bus two days in a row to the end of the road at Wonder Lake. The "mountain was out," and we were lucky to see it. We also saw bears, caribou, and a lone wolf. The bouncy ride in the old yellow school bus, and craning my neck to see out the window, was tough on my back, but we were really lucky with the beautiful, clear weather.

After Denali, we headed south all the way back to California through Alaska, Canada, and the northern states. We drove 2,500 miles in one week. Somewhere still in Alaska, I had back trouble that made it hard for me to sit up, so I lay on the bed in the back of the van until I got some painkillers in a remote town. Back problems were new to me, but probably brought on by sitting for many miles. Later, we finally saw a moose in a swamp in Canada after looking for one throughout Alaska. We enjoyed British Columbia and then angled over to Alberta, down through Jasper to Banff along the Icefield Parkway before crossing the border and heading home through swarms of Idaho mosquitoes and the dry western states. It felt good to be back in the lower forty-eight!

While we were in Alaska, Alison had been in the Ukraine with Peace Child, a group she traveled and performed with for about a month—both Ukrainian and American kids singing and acting together. She came home with lots of songs and stories. This was after the Chernobyl disaster of 1986, and I remember still being quite concerned about fallout, but Alison, of course, was not. She told me, "Well, I didn't eat any tomatoes!"

Alison started high school in September 1990 after we got married. We all settled into a routine, living in Mill Valley, but Roger stayed some weeknights in Livermore where he worked in nuclear weapons research as an engineer at Lawrence Livermore National Lab. We spent most of our weekends in Mill Valley, hiking and enjoying a good social life, but sometimes we went to Livermore and enjoyed wine tasting and hiking there as well. Alison spent some weekends and vacations with Jerry. Roger and I enjoyed both homes and would banter with each other, "You should never sell *your* house!" Roger had rented the upstairs in Livermore to a veterinarian so the place wouldn't sit empty, and she adopted Roger's aging cat George.

Alison and I had busy schedules. She was studying at Tamalpais High School as well as playing her clarinet as the only girl in a jazz band. I was now teaching third grade at Edna Maguire Elementary School—another Mill Valley school I had attended as a student for my middle school years. It had now been reopened as an elementary school with a huge school garden, and Strawberry School had been closed and rented out as office-and-warehouse space.

By this time Roger and Alison were developing a good relationship, with many discussions about school, friendships, and politics. Alison had several good friends by now, and Roger and I developed good friendships with them as well. Some of those friendships have lasted into her adulthood. We all enjoyed the outdoors together, often hiking on trails on Mount Tamalpais right out our front door. Sometimes we took Alison and friends on overnight trips to the mountains—once cross-country skiing with

Elizabeth Shafer at Lakes Basin, another time hiking with Jen Tenant in Yosemite, and also a backpacking trip to Point Reyes National Seashore with Jessica Posner. One year, we hosted a Russian exchange student briefly, and another time, a French student for a month in August.

By now, Alison was in the high school orchestra as well as the Marin Youth Symphony Orchestra. I drove her to regular lessons and rehearsals, and Roger always gladly joined me in attending her concerts. Near the end of her senior year we proudly watched her as a soloist performing the Mozart Clarinet Concerto with the Marin Youth Symphony Orchestra. For weeks at home, we had enjoyed hearing the music coming upstairs from her bedroom as she practiced. I had started her on Suzuki piano lessons when she was four and she needed lots of nudging and supervision to practice, but by high school, she was an accomplished musician inspiring herself to succeed. That success took her all the way through college.

Three years after our wedding, Roger got a good retirement package and decided to leave Lawrence Livermore Lab. He was fifty-six and ready to enjoy retirement. He always had a renter upstairs in Livermore and enjoyed being back in his old hometown. Mill Valley had been a wonderful place in which to grow up, and we discovered that we had both lived in the same canyon, I at 78 Coronet Avenue, he at 168 Woodbine. Because he was six years older than I, our lives had never crossed. Now we were living just a few houses down the hill from where his uncle Horace had lived and also not far from his cousin Patty.

At this time, Roger's mother was still living in Mill Valley at 16 Montford Avenue, and his father on Bethel Island in the Delta. My father had died, but my mother still lived in Marinwood, San Rafael, at 613 Idylberry Road. Sometimes we all got together in Mill Valley for holidays. Valerie and Cameron occasionally visited us there too, but most of their holidays were spent with their mother, Anna, in Livermore.

After Roger retired, we got a dog at the Marin Humane Society—a very anxious golden retriever who was about one and a half years old. At times, we wondered what we had done. We had to blockade ourselves to sit on our couch or eat dinner, or we had to put him in a training crate to get peace of mind. In the long run, Ben turned out to be the best dog anyone could hope for. He was loved by everyone. In Mill Valley, Roger walked downtown daily for coffee, and Ben made instant friends; Roger, never being at a loss for words, did so also. Later, when we moved out to Livermore, Ben was so loved by the Masons next door that they also took care of him when we traveled, and he never went to a kennel in his life. The parents, Jamie and Jeff, always reported on his early morning "help" when the kids were getting ready for school and he paraded around the house carrying their socks in his mouth. Lucky dog and lucky all of us. He lived to be seventeen and is buried and memorialized by a plaque on our property. His death was a huge blow, and we still miss him.

When I met Roger, he was actively doing white water canoeing and kayaking through Outdoors Unlimited at UCSF and a club called POST, which was based in Oakland. Both of these groups canoed and kayaked year-round on rivers and lakes. Soon after we met, Roger helped me pick out a Kiwi kayak and equipment, and we headed straight for an easy run on the Russian River. I loved being in nature in a new way—on the water. Alison and I both wanted to learn how to canoe, so Roger took us to canoeing classes at UCSF. There, in a pool, we learned strokes and how to maneuver the canoe and get back in if we fell out in a river. Being so young and light, Alison popped herself right back in; it was more of a challenge for me, but I mastered it too, though it took all the upper-body strength I could muster. After our training, we started going on many river trips with the POST club. (The leader, Bill Hitchings had originally formed the club as a Boy Scout post when his boys were young, and the name stuck when he continued the club for adults.)

With POST, Roger, Alison, and I made many canoe trips over the next several years. The club had a passenger van that pulled a trailer for the canoes and kayaks. There was one trip a month—usually overnight camping trips, often with a central camp we'd return to each night, but sometimes canoe camping along a river. We always had a central commissary and shared the cooking and cleaning chores. It was very well organized, humorous, and lively. There were several very talented and great people on these trips. I usually did tandem canoeing with Roger, but sometimes Alison paddled with Roger, and I with Bill Hitchings, Don Jarrell, or others. Alison and I had less experience, so a strong boater in the stern for steering was important, but we were learning fast.

In the winters and spring, we canoed rivers such as the Navarro, Trinity, Stanislaus, Tuolumne, Russian, and Cache Creek. One time, on the Trinity River, Alison was kayaking alone, and we were canoeing tandem nearby. She got pinned sideways above water on a big boulder and called out, "What do I do now?" She was in no danger, but it was a funny moment that I can still picture. She also lost a Teva sandal in that rapid, so the club thereafter called it "Lost Teva Rapid" in her honor. One leader, Don Jarrell, would occasionally spot old, abandoned tires along a river and shout out "for Alison's car" after her dad bought her a Toyota. One time in Oregon, I was paddling in the bow and didn't realize that Roger had fallen out of the stern as we took a corner, so I just kept going. I didn't get far because other club members were waving me down. When paddling in rapids, you can't always hear above the noise of the river. We always had a lot of humor mixed in with the excitement on those trips, and there were no end of jokes and stories over dinner and wine in camp each night.

In the summers, we took longer trips to Oregon, Idaho, and Montana, traveling and camping. Our dog Ben was always welcome on the trips; he had his own lifejacket and traveled down low in the bottom of the canoe with his nose over the edge. Only one time did he jump out in a rapid, and I only knew that when I heard Roger behind me saying, "Damn dog!" as he grabbed him by the handle on his lifejacket and hauled him back into the boat, and we paddled on down the river.

Another time, we were all circled around a campfire along the Carson River in Nevada, and Ben became a lapdog as he moved around the circle from lap to lap, never touching the ground. It helped that everyone had been drinking plenty of wine and didn't mind a large damp, sandy dog in their laps. Alison was always a welcome participant and well admired because she was good company and becoming a skilled boater, even though she was the only teenager among adults. Everyone was really kind and encouraging. On one trip to Oregon, there were only a few of us in the van, and Alison read six paperback books. When she finished them, she started them over. I still picture her sitting in the canoe on shore at lunchtime in her wetsuit with her legs hanging over the side and her nose in a book.

Roger and I continued boating with POST for several years until his knees and my shoulder began to complain. Then, for calmer trips, we paddled with friends for eight days down the muddy Green River, through Canyonlands National Park to the confluence with the Colorado—calm water and easy paddling. Before the trip, we purchased khaki clothes at the Goodwill Store, wore them over our swimsuits, and threw them away at the end of the muddy trip. At first, Roger and I were going too fast ahead of the others because we were so used to whitewater canoeing; then we realized that I could relax and read the guidebook in the bow, and he could steer from the rear, just letting the slow current carry us along. Our group of about eight friends camped along the way; the scenery was spectacular and the company wonderful. We cooked for each other and shared the chores each night. As we drifted along, we were surrounded by tall, red sandstone cliffs accented by blue skies with beautiful clouds, and we were surprised by new scenes around each bend in the river. We were learning to relax on rivers.

Another year, we went with the same group to Montana and spent eight days floating on the Marias and Missouri Rivers in Lewis and Clark country. Again, we experienced beautiful scenery, friendship, and historical areas as we floated. We camped where Lewis and Clark had been, and alongside the river, we saw bones from a Native American buffalo jump imbedded in the river bank. For each of these trips, our friend, John Rundberg, from Seattle gathered the maps and made the arrangements for shuttles at the beginning and end of each trip. He is a man who loves to live the life of an old explorer; he makes his own canoes, cooks in dutch ovens, works with leather, and keeps daily journals. We were very fortunate to share these experiences with him, and we still enjoy phone conversations a few times a year.

Roger and I had both traveled and lived abroad before we met, but now traveling in California and the West was very appealing. Roger had attended the University of Nevada in Reno, and we both loved the long views in the high desert and the smell of sage. One winter we went to the low desert of Death Valley, where I had been so many times, and we camped out of the back of our Ford truck covered by a fiberglass shell. Nights in Death Valley in the winter can be very cold, and one of our nights at the Furnace Creek Campground the temperature dropped to seventeen degrees, freezing water in a plastic cup by our campfire. We froze in the truck and stayed in a motel the next night to thaw out. Luckily, the days were sunny and bright, and we enjoyed our time in the valley.

That was just the first of many trips to Death Valley in the winter season, but by then, we had learned to always take the right gear. Over the years, we camped in tents, trucks, and RVs, and now we often spoil ourselves and enjoy the comfort of motels with showers and soft beds. Occasionally, we still feel the urge to camp and occasionally do so in good weather and remote areas. Twice in the spring season we were lucky to see super blooms when the desert floor and alluvial fans are covered with wildflowers. These usually occur about every ten years, only when the conditions permit, and we saw them in both 2005 and 2015. Even in other years, we have often gone to see flowers and cacti in bloom in March or April, and I photograph these scenes now with a lightweight digital camera, not the cumbersome cameras I used to use. I still have many good black-and-white prints from my previous days in the valley.

In those early years together, Roger and I escaped from our jobs as time permitted and visited several national parks and scenic areas. We stayed in campgrounds, but sometimes backpacked for a few days. One summer we took our canoe on top of our truck to Utah and did a two-day run down the San Juan River, just the two of us camping out. It was so hot at night we didn't even need our sleeping bags, just crawled into our tent above the river to escape high winds and blowing sand and slept all night on mats, with our heads on stuffed sleeping bags for pillows. The next morning was calm and beautiful, surrounded by towering cliffs. We were visited by a family of ptarmigans as we ate breakfast by the quietly flowing river.

Back on the river, we ran the only significant rapid after asking some other boaters to watch us go through safely. That afternoon the wind came up again just before we pulled ashore at Mexican Hat. Roger helped me turn over the canoe on shore and secure everything so it wouldn't blow away. Then he hiked up to a prearranged spot to call for our shuttle from Recapture Lodge in Bluff. While I waited onshore with the canoe, I crawled under some tamarisk trees for protection from the hot wind. Later, back at the lodge, we left our muddy, squishy water sandals and dirty clothes outside the door of our room. A shower and air-conditioned shelter never felt so good.

A couple of times we backpacked in the Grand Canyon and camped at the Colorado River level at Phantom Ranch five thousand feet below the rim. I had hiked there many times before and should have remembered to trim my toenails for the descent, but on the first trip with Roger, I didn't follow my own good advice and got blisters under both big toenails as we pounded down the trail with our toes hitting up against the front of our boots. Back at home, I wore open-toed sandals for several months as the nails grew back in.

Alison traveled with her dad on several occasions when he went to conferences abroad. They went to China when she was in middle school, and she rode a bicycle through Tiananmen Square with Chinese students, ate exotic foods, and traveled up the Yangtze River on a tour boat with her dad. Another summer she went to Germany with Jerry, her half brother Chris, and Jerry's wife, Barbara, who had relatives there. Alison also visited England and Canada a few times to see her Canadian relatives in British Columbia. In 1990, she had gone to the Ukraine with Peace Child.

Now, in her junior year in 1993, she and her friend Elizabeth Shafer, along with the principal and the Russian teacher, participated in the high school's first Russian Club visit to Moscow. They were housed with families and treated to special dinners. She was able to speak a little Russian and came home with good stories and colorful lacquer souvenirs. It was a short visit, and we returned the hospitality a year later by hosting a Russian student in our home for a week. At the end of that visit, we were astonished to see the girl's Russian escort/teacher cramming everything she could into her own suitcases at the airport. She wanted to toss out the gifts we had given to our visiting student and replace them with her things! A diplomatic struggle ensued (with no shared language), and we hoped our student arrived home with her Levi's skirt and Keds for her brother.

Finally, in her senior year, Alison was accepted to colleges. We were on another backpacking trip in the Grand Canyon with Alison when the anticipated acceptance letters were to arrive. It had been a hard decision for her to leave home at that time, but we arranged for my colleague and good neighbor, Christy Herrmann, to open the mail when we called home on our return trip. Then, by chance, we had to hurry home because I developed a toothache in the bottom of the Grand Canyon. So, standing at a payphone outside a Jack-in-the Box in Needles, California, at the California/Arizona border, we got the good news; Alison had been accepted to Princeton, Stanford, UC Berkeley, UC San Diego, and UC Davis! We were really excited and hurried home to enjoy the good news.

After Alison's acceptances, it was time to make a choice about where she would go. Roger and she toured Stanford while I was working, and then she flew on her own to Princeton for an orientation. When she came home a few days later, we picked her up at the Marin Airporter bus in Mill Valley, and she hopped off wearing a Princeton sweatshirt. She had decided; now we had to convince her dad, Jerry. He wanted her to attend UC Berkeley; he was right that she could get a very good undergraduate education there and then go to a more expensive school for graduate work, but Alison really wanted to go to Princeton, and I wanted her to have the experience of going away to college, living on campus and getting exposed to a new environment. Jerry was right about the finances, for which he was mainly responsible. We already had saved up enough for four years at Berkeley, but we would need loans for Princeton. Jerry finally agreed. He paid the bulk with savings and loans, I sent monthly spending money, Alison worked part-time on campus, and he and Alison finally paid off the accrued loans several years later, with few regrets because she did so well.

In August 1994, Alison and I flew to Newark, New Jersey, had a day visiting sites in New York City, and then rented a car and drove to Princeton. Our first mistake was missing the on-ramp for the turnpike and ending up on surface streets in Elizabeth, New Jersey, where we locked the doors and viewed the poverty. Finally, we made it to Princeton where we stayed with our British friends Phil and Ruth Holmes, who had visited us in Scotland when Alison was a baby in 1977. Phil was now teaching at Princeton and was still a colleague of Jerry's, but I had not seen them since our divorce. We had a lovely time together before I needed to return home to begin the school year in Mill Valley.

Before leaving, I was able to see Alison's dorm room, tour campus, attend a concert, and shop for dorm supplies, but Phil and Ruth moved her into the dorm and met her two roommates a few days later. When I left, saying goodbye was harder on me than Alison. I was choking back the tears when we hugged, and she was saying, "Oh, Mom, you'll be okay." I cried after I drove away, but stopped and calmed myself before negotiating the turnpike back to the airport. There, I ate a lonely, delicious slice of pizza and boarded my plane. The whole experience seemed so strange, but good at the same time. I was so proud of Alison, but at home, I closed the door to her bedroom until I was used to her being gone. This preceded the days of cell phones and texting. Dial-up phones had to be used, so a dorm-mate would holler down the hall so I could speak to her.

Since his children were older, Roger had already been through what I was now experiencing, and I appreciated his understanding. Life for us returned to a new norm, and we continued with our usual activities. That first fall, Alison spent Thanksgiving at Cape Cod with my friend Mary Ellen Ackerman from our Death Valley days. She finally returned home at Christmas and then again the next summer of 1995. That summer we hosted her roommates, Margie and Deborah, for a visit in Mill Valley. We took them camping at Steep Ravine above the coast where the fog rolled in but didn't dampen our spirits. Neither had done much camping before, but we kept them warm by a campfire, and we heard entertaining laughter from their tent. They had turned out to be wonderful roommates—Margie from Greenwich, Connecticut, and Deborah from the "only Asian family" in Laramie, Wyoming, where her father taught at the university. Princeton had done a great job matching them up as roommates.

At home, my interest doing serious photography was waning. I had become very busy with my job, enjoying Alison's activities, but not long darkroom hours. I wanted to spend time with Roger, our friends, and outdoor activities without the burden of heavy photo equipment or the long hours in the darkroom. I've always had a darkroom, but even today I don't spend time there. Now I always carry a small pocket camera or a digital SLR. With relief and delight, I recall a humorous remark that Imogen Cunningham had made to me, "What the world really needs is more gardeners." I get it! Put your hands into the soil and find peace and beauty that gardening can bring. In my life, the same could be said of hiking, horseback riding, boating, and getting out in nature. That's where I find peace and happiness.

With Alison at college, Roger and I lived in Mill Valley, where I continued teaching for two more years. We hiked locally on Mount Tamalpais, and I often hiked over the ridge to and from my school. In his retirement, he enjoyed hiking with the local Sierra and Alpine Clubs. Once or twice, he went to Utah on hiking trips, and often cross-country skiing, staying at the Alpine Club lodge near Echo Pass. I joined him when I could, but didn't begrudge him going when I couldn't. He had worked for thirty years and had earned his retirement. I knew I still had responsibilities with a daughter in college, and I needed to work until I could comfortably retire.

By this time, I was teaching third grade. A retired teacher had once told me she loved teaching third graders because they "love their teachers!" This seemed very true to me, and we had a lot of fun in the classroom. I enjoyed teaching everything—especially music, art, and science. In my classroom I had a guinea pig named Olga da Polga, after a childhood book of Alison's that I read to my class every year. Olga lived to be eleven years old, rare for a guinea pig, and was loved by the whole school. We celebrated her birthday every year, with lettuce cakes and carrot candles. Funny that I was so heartbroken when she died my principal sent me home for the day to grieve.

In my classroom, a parent helped me develop a fish hatchery for raising steelhead trout. To simulate a cold stream, he put a glass aquarium inside an old refrigerator, put a Plexiglas window in the door, and brought us tiny fish eggs from the hatchery in Sonoma County. For six weeks every spring, we watched the fish hatch and grow into fingerlings, and I designed curriculum that included art, writing, math (prediction of hatching dates), and environmental awareness. At the end of six weeks, we took a field trip to the hatchery area where we were required to return the fingerlings to their native stream. On the first field trip, we boarded a school bus, but the driver surprised us, after all the kids were loaded, when she referred to the fish in a bucket and said we could not bring "pets" on the bus. What? The father helping us had to drive them north in his car. After that, we always drove the kids and fish in cars.

I was teaching when the Golden Gate Bridge turned fifty, and I developed a curriculum about the bridge that I used every year, knowing that it was important local history. Each year my students did wonderful large detailed drawings of the bridge, accurately showing the towers and cables, boats underneath, clouds and birds overhead. One year I had a parent who worked for the bridge come to share her information about bridge workers, showing the gear they wore, including all the safety slings, helmets, and carabiners.

At school we also had a huge school garden where our students learned basic skills, such as composting, and using garden tools to plant and harvest crops that we would sell at our own farmers' markets once a week. The staff built a whole curriculum around the garden, including science, writing, reading, and math. I worked with a wonderful staff, several of whom I still see socially today twenty years later.

After Alison's second year at Princeton, I decided to rent out our house in Mill Valley and take a leave of absence from my job for a year. Even though I really enjoyed my work, it came with all the stresses of full-time teaching—curriculum planning, meetings, parent conferencing, and a demanding schedule. At this time, I was fifty-three and two years away from the earliest possibility of retirement at age fifty-five. But the real reason I wanted to leave was that Roger had been retired for three years, and there were many things we wanted to do together. I was lucky to have this choice and glad the Mill Valley School District agreed to the leave for one year.

One year turned to two as I tried out country life in Livermore. After those two years, I retired. Then, I did substitute teaching in Livermore that first year until I felt that the finances were working out. I had no trouble renting my house in Mill Valley at a rate that nearly equaled my teacher's salary or I wouldn't have considered leaving my job. Previous to this decision, we had been telling each other, "You shouldn't sell your house; it's too special." For two years, we kept both places, but I finally sold my house because I no longer wanted to deal with maintenance costs and rental issues. I had also been concerned, for Alison's sake, about leaving the family home in Mill Valley, but when I asked her how she felt, she sweetly said, "Mom, I am fine with anything as long as you are still in the Bay Area!"

During this time, my mother still lived in San Rafael, and my brother moved from the Sausalito waterfront to Petaluma. My mom did well living alone for twenty years after my father's death. She enjoyed her garden, reading, and shopping. And she enjoyed smoking and her evening scotch almost until the day she died at age ninety-one. She never wanted to join senior activities or socialize with others. She lived simply and didn't seem lonely, even in her old age. She aged as a very self-contained, reserved person, enjoying her solitude. After a long life of socializing, arranging family activities, and preparing beautiful company dinners for my father's colleagues, she seemed to enjoy simplicity. For many years, I often drove from Livermore to see her once a week. After choking on cigarette smoke all my life, I finally got up the nerve to ask her to not smoke in my presence, and she willingly went into her bedroom or outside after that. Had I only asked earlier!

My brother, Larry, lived on the Sausalito waterfront until he was in his fifties. He had been married to my high school friend Francie Oman, and they had one son, Colin. They divorced after seven years, but Colin often lived with him in Sausalito. Larry designed trimarans and ferro-cement sailboats, and they lived in one of his forty-two-foot boats for many years anchored offshore, occasionally tied at a dock. He had named the boat after our grandfather, C. A. Marcy. He also was an expert at repairing heavy marine engines. Years later, and after several bouts of winter pneumonia, he changed his lifestyle and moved ashore to Petaluma in Sonoma County. He got a job driving buses with the Golden Gate Transit system to and from San Francisco, and also in western Marin County. After steering large boats for many years, he seemed an expert at handling large buses, and often won awards for his maneuvering at the practice bus rodeos held by the company. After growing up with a brother who had always been so capable at anything mechanical, I was not surprised.

The summer of 1996, when Alison came home from Princeton, she, Roger, and I planned our move to Livermore and then to spend a month backpacking the whole 211-mile John Muir Trail. Early summer, we moved all the furniture, books and belongings to Livermore until all we had left in the Mill Valley house was backpacking food lined up for each week on the empty living room bookshelves. Then we packed some of it in five-gallon plastic tubs to send as caches for pickup in two places along the trail: Red's Meadow Resort near Mammoth Lakes and Muir Trail Ranch farther south near Florence Lake. We would leave from Yosemite Valley at Happy Isles, a rocky spot on the Merced River, and arrive eventually at the top of Mount Whitney

On August 3, 1996, we drove to the Yosemite Valley floor, checked in at the ranger station with our prearranged permit, and camped in the backpackers' campground. We had one three-person tent and what we thought was minimal gear and food. Very early the next morning, we parked our car in the long-term parking area and hiked to the trailhead. After a quick photo shoot, we started the hike—uphill for two days to Tuolumne Meadows, a distance of twenty miles. Our first night was at Sunrise Creek where we met a honeymoon couple who had been married the day before at the fancy Ahwahnee Hotel in Yosemite Valley. They chased off bears by clanging pots eight times overnight, but were ready to go the next morning. We would see them a couple of more times on the trail, and would receive a note from them on our food cache many miles later at Muir Trail Ranch.

Roger, Alison, and I trudged on with heavy packs to Tuolumne Meadows—two days sporting blisters and sore backs. Alison was already out-hiking us at times and encouraged us to drop some nonessential items at Tuolumne. Roger met a gal on the trail who wanted to hike to the valley floor, and we needed our car at Tuolumne to dump extra stuff, so he traded our car keys with her so he could drive her car to the valley floor and she could hike down. Then he would retrieve our car and drive back up to meet us. Alison and I used the time to sort out extra stuff and relax. We had many years of backpacking experience but never a monthlong trip, and we needed to pare down the weight. With Alison's encouragement, we did that. We had started with forty-five pound packs, but they were too heavy. When Roger returned, we hit the trail again, with lighter packs, and continued out the Lyell Fork of the Tuolumne River for several miles. Soon I caught a bootlace from one boot on my other boot's brass clasp and fell flat on my face, pack and all, picked myself up, and off, we went, glad that I was still in one piece. That night a cigarette lighter left by someone in our campfire pit exploded, and that didn't faze us either, so we were off to a good start.

The three of us hiked together for eight days, all the way to Red's Meadow Pack Station, which is the only place the JMT meets a road, and where we had sent our first food cache. Those first sixty miles go through some of Yosemite's most beautiful backcountry—over Donohue Pass and passing Mount Lyell, Banner Peak, Mount Ritter, the Minarets, Thousand Island, and Garnet Lakes. We had perfect weather. When we arrived at Red's Meadow, we decided to return home with Alison, rather than continuing. Alison was missing her friends, and Roger and I had new backpacks that were very uncomfortable. Sitting in the café for lunch at Red's Meadow, Roger, in his usual friendly way, asked out loud if anyone knew how we could get back to Tuolumne Meadows to get our car. Well, a very nice older guy spoke up, inviting us to stay overnight at his condo in Mammoth Lakes, enjoy a nice dinner with his French friends whom he was touring around, and they would drive Roger to Tuolumne Meadows the next morning when they continued their sightseeing. So within a few hours, we were soaking in a hot tub and sleeping in comfortable beds. Not a bad consequence for changing our plans.

Later that summer, in early September after Alison had returned to school, Roger and I returned to the JMT and headed south for eight days. At my request, we started hiking on the first day of school—freedom for me! Again, we found a hiker, this time Felix, who had completed the JMT eleven times and would take our car keys north to Red's Meadow, retrieve our car and park it for us at South Lake and the Bishop Pass trailhead. Near there, at a T intersection in Le Conte Canyon, we found his note telling us where our car was parked. He had also washed the car and left some of his extra supplies inside for us. We were learning about the camaraderie and friendship of perfect strangers on the trail.

Over the next three summers, Roger and I completed our rugged hike of the whole John Muir Trail by summiting Mount Whitney and then gorging down greasy hamburgers at the Whitney Portal café at trail's end far below. We had finally experienced the whole trail—the spectacular granite peaks, the high lakes and passes, and the lush alpine meadows.

Alison graduated from Princeton in 1998 with a degree in mechanical engineering. Roger and I flew to New Jersey for the graduation and enjoyed visiting New York City as well as the campus. There were festive graduation activities before and after the ceremony. Jerry and Alison's boyfriend, Mitchell Mutz, also came for the impressive outdoor ceremony that was under a shaded area surrounded by ivy-covered buildings. Jerry treated us all to dinner afterward at a nearby Chinese restaurant, and then we all went to the dance. One afternoon we watched the "P"rade march through campus, a parade done yearly with members of each class represented in order of oldest first to current grads last. The costumes, laughter, and music made it delightful to watch. Then, that night, we all sat on a big grass field and witnessed a huge fireworks show, one of the most impressive I have ever seen. (In June 2018, Alison and her family returned for her twentieth reunion, and they all marched in the "P"rade.)

After graduation, we all returned to California—Roger and I to Livermore and Alison and Mitch to live together in Palo Alto. By this time, they had dated for about two years, beginning at Princeton where they had met in the orchestra. Mitch had been living there while finishing his dissertation in biochemistry from University of Rochester because his adviser had moved there. He was twelve years older than Alison and had lived abroad playing professional horn with the Stuttgart Opera Orchestra before deciding to return to university for his PhD. We had liked Mitchell immediately when we met him the previous summer. A good-looking, fun-loving, talented and warm person, we were happy to see their relationship growing.

By this time, Alison had been accepted for graduate school in mechanical engineering at Stanford. Mitch already had a job in Palo Alto, and they rented a cottage in the College Terrace area on Oberlin Street, coincidentally the same street where my parents had lived when they were newlyweds in the 1930s. (My mother was still living in San Rafael at this time, but couldn't remember the address so we were never able to figure out which house they had rented.) Alison and Mitch's cottage was owned by a retired man named Art who had his colorful model train set up in the garage next to their cottage behind his house. They all became friends and enjoyed time together.

Two years later, Alison and Mitch married September 3, 2000, at the Lawrence Hall of Science in Berkeley. The hall is in the hills high above campus, and as a small child, Alison had always pronounced it the "Lower Hall of Science." The wedding was imaginative with its science theme, and about 150 guests came from near and far. There were many family members, as well as their childhood and university friends. It had been quite a project to plan and put together, but when I sat down for the formal dinner in the large hall, with the low lighting of planets and stars overhead, I felt a glow of happiness.

Three years later, Alison and Mitch bought their first house in Mountain View, just south of Palo Alto. It was a really nice, one-story, three-bedroom house on a sunny lot in a friendly neighborhood. They ripped out the rugs and, with some instruction from Roger, started laying down wood floors immediately. I was happy to see that the family remodeling projects were now transferred to the younger generation.

Through all of this, Alison continued her graduate studies at Stanford, then followed by a postdoctoral position in the field of pediatric cardiology—a field that she continues to work in today. In 2005, Alison and Mitch had their first child, Eliza Ferne Mutz, on June 28, 2005, at Packard Children's Hospital at Stanford. Three years later, they moved to San Diego where Alison accepted her first job as an assistant professor at UC San Diego. At first, they rented a condo in La Jolla, but within a year, bought a house on the hill above town. Our grandson, Isaac Marsden Mutz, was welcomed into the family on May 5, 2008, in San Diego. Mitch continued working in his own biotech company, Amplex, which he had moved to La Jolla. Over the years, Roger and I enjoyed many trips to La Jolla and lots of visits to Balboa Park where we saw the San Diego Zoo and the many museums. La Jolla was a wonderful place to raise small children. However, in 2015, when Alison was hired as an associate professor at Stanford by the Departments of Pediatric Cardiology and Bioengineering, the whole family moved north again and settled into a house they bought on the Stanford campus. Mitch continued commuting twice monthly to his company in La Jolla, but eventually got a new job as investment director with Roche Pharmaceuticals housed at Genentech in South San Francisco. I am incredibly proud of them both and how they handle all the comings and goings of their lives. They always strive for a good balance of hard work and fun for both themselves and their children. As much as we all loved La Jolla, it has been really nice to live closer again so we can share family time.

When I met Roger, his kids were in their twenties. Valerie had been in the army in Germany, but came back to Livermore in 1990 after divorcing her husband. She settled down in Livermore, where she had grown up, got a job, and resumed old friendships. Eventually, she went back to school to earn her BA at Cal State Hayward. When she turned thirty, she held a big party with music and tie-dying in our backyard. A few years later, Val was in a domestic partnership with her friend, Sheri Morris, who is a doctor at Kaiser. They lived together, bought their first house in Livermore, and they, too, did a lot of remodeling. Then, through a successful experience with IVF and donor sperm, Val had their first child—our first grandchild, Miles Cameron Thomey Morris, on April 18, 2005, in Walnut Creek. Two years later, our granddaughter Jada Sage Thomey Morris was also born (same donor) in Walnut Creek on June 9, 2007. It is fun to note that she was born on Alison's birthday. Later, Val and Sheri moved to another larger house where we enjoyed a lot of family holidays. Sadly, things didn't work out for them, and they went through a difficult separation in 2014. Since their divorce, they have shared custody and have continued to raise two beautiful children. Now, they live in separate homes that are close enough so the kids can walk or bike between houses.

Roger's son, Cameron, continues to live in the Los Angeles area where he is still pursuing work in video production and many other promotional and advertising projects. He is a creative worker, an impressive photographer, and never lacking ideas for good projects. Cameron enjoys sports, including tennis, golf, and cycling, and often travels to the mountains for hiking and climbing. He is also very active with his nephew and niece, Miles and Jada, and their friends.

He has been married and divorced, but always has an upbeat attitude and easily finds new like-minded friends.

Our grandchildren are very special people, developing their own interests and activities. Eliza is an excellent student and works very hard. She is also an equestrian, choral singer, a reader, and is very sociable. She has her own horse, and also participates in the Interscholastic Equestrian Association (IEA) for junior high school students at Stanford's Red Barn. Isaac is also a very good student, a budding pianist, and now starting trumpet in school band. I have always noticed that he is observant in nature, knows cars, and is very kind and gentle with animals. He's good at soccer and tennis and loves to hike. Miles is creative with Legos, drawing, and computers, and is very helpful and kind. He is also capable with tools and may end up like his Grandpa Roger someday. Jada has a wonderful spirit and loves to dance, swim, do gymnastics, and sing with her Karaoke machine. She's fair-minded, humorous, and independent. We are lucky that the grandchildren are close enough in age to play together when we have gatherings at our ranch or at their homes. We always remark that they get along very well even though they don't see each other that often.

A very difficult time for us occurred in 2013 when I helped my brother, Larry, through a bone marrow transplant at Stanford Hospital. Even though he was a Kaiser patient, he was referred to Stanford for treatment. I agreed to be his caregiver for three months, living in an apartment with him close to the BMT clinic and hospital. This was a very hard period for Roger and me because Roger stayed at home and traveled back and forth to see us on weekends. Unfortunately, those three months stretched to five because Larry developed other life-threatening issues—surgery on an enlarged pituitary gland, and later some skin cancer issues. The BMT clinic had wonderful doctors and nurses, and we made some very nice friends. With all the good care, Larry survived and is still living five years later cancer-free. After my time away, it was wonderful for me to be home with Roger as we resumed our lives and continued our adventures.

In Livermore, we have seven acres of pasture land. When he was young, Roger had packed in the mountains and had owned horses. When I met him, he told me that if we ever wanted to ride, we should just pay for day rides in the mountains. I had rarely ridden a horse, but I had hiked with donkeys in the mountains and thought it would be fun to have one for carrying our packs when we hiked. Amazingly, Roger was willing to indulge in my donkey fantasy, so we started looking for one to buy.

One day, at the local feed store, we ran into our friend Marilyn Russell who said, "Take my old horse; you can pack him." She was talking about Centur, her retired endurance horse who was eighteen by then, but still in great shape. With Marilyn, he had completed five thousand miles of endurance races over the years.

I was fifty-three years old and had never owned a horse, but thought, *Why not?* and Roger was experienced and willing. Marilyn and I agreed to an arrangement where we could both change our minds. So within a few days, I had Centur in the pasture, and I learned which end to feed and how to groom. Soon, I was taking lessons from our friend Jean Schreiber. I had the usual fears of a beginner and was sure the horse might run away with me, but he never did. He was very obedient and experienced, and very patient as he taught me how to ride. I ended up riding Centur for four years on many local and mountain trails, but as he aged, I needed a younger animal.

Eventually, I ended up buying a riding mule, Georgia Peach, who carried me for nearly ten years. I had always loved "long ears," and Georgia became available from a friend of ours. After safely trying her on steep trails, and watching her happy, floppy ears, I was ready to own a mule. Roger was given Jake, a quarter horse, that he rode for several years, but eventually his main horse became Buddy, which he purchased on a whim at an auction. Buddy was a rascal when he was young, but Roger persisted, had him trained, and they became a wonderful pair on the trails. I admit there were many times when I thought Roger would get tossed off, but he stuck to the saddle and never got hurt. My mule Georgia and I would often watch from behind on the trail while they sorted things out.

Together, and with friends, Roger and I had many adventures on horse- and mule-back. We rode the entire Tahoe Rim Trail, a 165-mile route high above Lake Tahoe, and away from crowds. Six of us rode that trail in sections over four summers, finally receiving certificates of completion from the Tahoe Rim Trail Association. Even Buddy and Georgia received certificates as the forty-fourth and forty-fifth animals to ever complete the trail. I guess they were counted in with the dogs and llamas.

For fifteen summers, we attended the Twain Harte Horsemen's High Sierra Ride and Campout at Eagle Meadows near Sonora Pass. There was always a large group of about a hundred campers gathered for day rides and summer meals under open-air tents at about seven thousand feet. It was a wonderful site with many trails to choose from, and great views of the surrounding mountains. Roger and I learned all the trails; our favorites were all-day rides out to Long Valley, another over to Cooper Meadow, and a steep ride to the Bennett Juniper Tree, and then up to the high point of Cowboy Heaven. There were shorter rides downhill to see flowers in Eagle Meadow, and out to an overlook from which you could see north to the prominent ridge of the Dardanelles. We knew the trails so well we often led group rides for the club.

In the fall of 2005, we rode in the Death Valley Ride, a six-day ride that stretched from Ridgecrest, California, through Trona, the Slate Range, across Panamint Valley, up Goler Wash, over Mengel Pass into Butte Valley, down into Death Valley, and up the West Side Road to Furnace Creek. This ride was organized each year by a club from Los Angeles. They trucked all our gear each day for the next campsite along the route and provided meals, porta-potties, showers, and a rolling bar they called the "goodie wagon." (We didn't partake knowing that riding and drinking don't go safely hand in hand.) We camped each night and rode about twenty-five miles a day in perfect weather for six days. We were given fancy silver buckles on completion.

Having lived in Death Valley, it was wonderful for me to revisit some of the remote areas from the saddle. Etched in my memory is a beautiful evening riding with Roger down from Warm Springs on Buddy and

Georgia in the moonlight, with only the valley and camp lights far in the distance on the West Side Road. We had ridden over thirty miles that day, and our butts were sore. But then, that night, I had the loudest argument of my life, nose to nose with a "cowboy" who had been drinking beer all day, and was now standing on the sidelines criticizing Roger's horse because he had kicked his horse the previous night when tied to the picket line.

As tired as I was, I still had a big voice and came forth with every swear word I could find as he tried to tie next to us while continuing his loud criticism. Why didn't he move to another spot? I'd had it; when pushed too hard, I snap and find my words. The next night, the camp boss made us a wonderful private picket line at our Eagle Borax campsite. Overall, it was a great trip with beautiful memories. A few years later, we met up with a guy who told the story without knowing it was us, and said, "Boy, did that guy's wife have a mouth on her!"

For several winters, Roger and I hauled Buddy and Georgia to Surprise, Arizona, to ride with friends who had a small three-acre dusty, but scenic, place they called the "Raunchy Rancho." We enjoyed day rides out into the desert and, one time, all the way up to the White Tanks where we had a huge view overlooking Surprise and Phoenix. Another time we went with them to Vulture Peak, and, on another occasion, trailered our mounts down to Cochise's Stronghold, where we camped and did day rides. We also rode and camped near Tucson at Catalina State Park where we saw eight rattlesnakes along the trail in *one* day, more than I had seen in my whole life. Luckily, they didn't rattle, and the horses didn't spook. That day, to sweeten the experience, we visited a huge petroglyph site that was shown to us by some other riders. There was no modern graffiti to ruin the symbols, and we were lucky to see it.

A few years later, I bought another small mule, Taco, and sent him to a good mule trainer in Tucson, Arizona. Three months later, Roger and I drove our horse trailer south to pick him up and drive him home via San Diego where we would visit Alison and the family. By phone, Alison helped us arrange an overnight stop at the county fairgrounds in Yuma, Arizona. We arrived in the dark, lined up our trailer alongside the barn, and put Taco in a stall where he was happy to stretch for the night. We, however, had a miserable night. It turned out there was an airport nearby with planes coming and going all night. And it was so hot we couldn't sleep a wink in our living quarters in the front of the trailer. I got out naked in the dark and showered under the hose. Luckily, we were the only people there that night, but I was so hot I doubt I would have cared if anyone had seen me. The next morning, we continued our trip to cooler San Diego.

From 2011 through 2015, we rode on the six-day mule rides in Yosemite National Park. We were lucky each time to go with Sheridan King, a legendary Yosemite wrangler who guided in the backcountry for more than thirty years. The six-day ride makes a sixty-five-mile loop in the high country of Yosemite, staying each night in the High Sierra Camps—Glen Aulin, May Lake, Sunrise, Merced Lake, and Vogelsang (the highest at ten thousand feet). These are rustic camps where you sleep in tent cabins and eat hearty meals in central dining halls. We were joined by our daughters, Val and Alison, on two of the trips. Val and I started the family tradition of swimming at every camp no matter how cold or shallow the water was, and we followed through each year. Our ten-year-old granddaughter, Eliza, joined us in 2015. We all did well each year, but Eliza's accomplishment was amazing. She never complained, and rode beautifully on her assigned mule, Cash. She even made up lyrics to the familiar tune of Erie Canal —"I've got a mule; his name is Cash, fifteen miles to Vogelsang Pass ..."

In addition to the mule trips in Yosemite, we often visited Utah in the spring or fall for about five years as well. Twice, we rode mules, Bill and Leslie, on the Red Rock Ride, a large group ride organized each year by a family out of Tropic, Utah, right below Bryce National Park. With them we did different rides each day for six days—Bryce, Zion, North Rim of the Grand Canyon, as well as red rock country in the area. Our longest day was thirty-two miles down the Paria River from Cannonville to Highway 89 east of Kanab. We crisscrossed the river many times, with the wranglers pointing out where to avoid quicksand. At the end of the ride, they greeted us with ice cream and drinks followed later by mounds of hors d'oeuvres and a huge dinner.

Another group we rode with in Utah was Hondoo Rivers and Trails led by Pat Kearny and Ken Kerrer Jr., who took us on five-day rides in Capitol Reef National Park, Escalante Wilderness, and the remote area of the San Rafael Swell. On these trips, we camped with our small group of friends in the backcountry and enjoyed wonderful meals, conversation, and high-desert views of sandstone formations. One time, a huge hailstorm pounded on our tent after we crawled into bed, and we peeked out to see our landscape covered in white. Usually, we had spectacular star viewing and complete quiet at night, except for the sound of horses grazing their hay while tied on their high-lines. Often we rode to remote natural amphitheaters that had Indian petroglyphs, or we saw expansive views of red rock country laid out before us. In the springtime, we rode through blooming red bud trees, beautiful creeks, and heard the heart-grabbing descending songs of the canyon wrens, my favorite bird. We became very attached to the Utah red rock country, and the horses who went by the names of Tommy, Ben, Waylon, and Willie.

Over the years Roger and I continued to return to the Sierra Valley and Lakes Basin Recreation Area north of Truckee, California. We had each been there as teenagers before we knew each other, and felt lucky to be able to continue going there together. As a teenager, just out of high school, I had been a camp counselor at a Girl Scout camp outside of Sierraville, and had slept under the stars for six weeks the summer of 1961. Roger had gone to Long Lake with Scotty Mills's family for many summers, had packed horses carrying supplies to the cabin, and had become acquainted with the Marcus, Barker, and Sheridan families. We've all grown up now, and Roger and I have been going back together for more than twenty-five years.

In the mountains, we also visited our friends Scott and Deb Mills at their small cabin at Haskell Creek Summer Home Tract near Yuba Pass. It had been owned by Scott's mother, Katie, who originally encouraged Roger to go to the Lakes Basin Recreation Area with their family every summer. She was the inspiration and foundation for Roger's lifelong connection with that area of the mountains. We've been back to that cabin many times for Mills's family gatherings, enjoying barbecues and rustic candlelit dinners on the deck, all squeezed around a long plank table built by Scott many years ago. In the late summer of 2011, we shared a dinner on the deck with them. Scott was not feeling well, and I'll always remember his cheerful smile that evening. It was just a few weeks later that he died of a stroke. A large memorial service was held for him that fall at the Mill Valley Outdoor Art Club. Many mountain friends attended in addition to his family and old friends. Roger made wonderful remarks about growing up with Scotty and his family in Mill Valley and the Lakes Basin area.

During summers of the 1950s, Roger had also become well acquainted with other families who ran nearby lodges in the area. He eventually worked at Elwell Lakes Lodge for Drew Childs, who was the grandfather of Sugie Childs, who we still know today as Sugie Barker. John Barker was a member of the Marcus family who ran the Lower Camp in the area, as well as the cabin on Long Lake. Sugie and John married over forty-five years ago and still run Elwell Lakes Lodge, which Sugie inherited from her parents. It was built by her grandfather in the 1920s, and along with their son Jeremy, they have maintained its rustic charm. For many years they also owned Gold Lake Lodge nearby, and with expertise, restored it as well. Roger knew John and Sugie as children running around the lodges and lakes area.

Every summer, we are still very fortunate to return and enjoy many hours of conversation and recollection of old times when we were all young in the mountains. We gather for dinners in a large dining hall that is now used primarily by family and weekly potlucks for guests. From this dining hall, there is a spectacular view of Mount Elwell which we have all climbed many times in the past. Drinks at sunset on the porch before dinner have become an evening ritual. Conversation can last for several hours—ranging from lodge and lake history to politics and travel. In recent years, we have also traveled with John and Sugie to Death Valley during the winter season for off-road adventures into some of the remote mining areas there. We hope to go exploring with them to Grand Gulch, one of their favorite areas in Utah.

Another family Roger knew at the lakes were the Sheridans, who ran Lake Center Lodge. Their lodge no longer stands, but Roger and I both remember it in its heyday with kids playing volleyball, horseshoes, and swimming. They are another family with whom we are still connected, and for many years have attended an annual "Saint Paddy's Day in the Mountains" on August 17. The Sheridan family spend many days each August camping at Gold Lake. Over the years, they have led long hikes in the area followed by Irish Coffees and singing around a campfire in the evenings. One year, we did a "Twenty-one Lakes Hike," followed by an even longer one the next year. The idea was to swim in every lake. Each summer we used to camp with them, along with our dog Ben, who was jokingly more welcome than we were. If we arrived after dark, we would hear, "Well, Ben's here!" After a long evening of music and socializing, Ben used to get tired of partying and stare at our tent door so he could go to bed before we did. We would unzip the door, and he would happily go in by himself until we crawled in much later.

We love the area of the Sierra Valley so much that at one time we owned a house nearby in Calpine, but later a ten-acre parcel of land in Sierraville. We always took our horses and mules there and rode all the trails we could find. Those were wonderful years enjoying beautiful mountains and long views of the Sierra Valley (five thousand feet), which is sometimes referred to as the largest high-alpine valley in the United States. As much as we loved owning our own property there, we eventually sold it to cut down on the cost and work. Then we boarded our horses at the Graeagle Stables where we could either trailer them up the seven miles to the lake trails or ride out from the stable. Graeagle is an old lumber town that has red-and white buildings that now house small shops and galleries. There is also a store, gas station, and central park where art shows are held each summer. These areas have pulled us back for most of our adult lives. We love the hiking, riding, and lifelong friendships we have in the area. We hope to be hiking there well into old age.

Over the years, Roger and I usually explored the western states, sometimes on road trips, and other times trailering our horse and mule to rides. The shared love that Roger and I have for the West has sustained us for many years, but a few other trips grabbed our interest also. Most notably, we went to Africa in 2005 with our neighbors and friends, the Meyers and the Russells. The two-week safari was organized through the Lindsay Wildlife Museum in Walnut Creek, California. It was the trip of a lifetime. We flew first to London and then on to Nairobi, Kenya. It was an arduous journey with airline delays and cramped seating, but we arrived in good shape, and after one night in Nairobi, we were flown to Masa Mara National Park where we were housed in a fancy, open-air hotel high on a hill overlooking the Serengeti Plains. My first impression was walking to an overlook with a distant view of giraffes sauntering among acacia trees.

Each evening and early morning we were taken in vans to view wildlife. The vans had open-air tops so you could stand up to view and take photographs, surrounded by animals. We saw elephants, zebras, rhinos, wildebeests, warthogs, and cats, including an elusive leopard. One morning we were taken down to a river for a "hippo breakfast," where we were served on a long table near the river in full view of hippos both in the water and on the opposite shore. We also visited other parks, including Samburu and the Ngorongoro Crater in Tanzania. We traveled from park to park, seeing some of the local towns and people and the rough, potholed roads where the dirt shoulders were better to drive on than the pavement. We visited Mount Kenya National Park where we were awakened to view the watering hole at night, when animals came to drink.

Another adventurous trip was to Katmai National Park in Alaska. We were invited and hosted by my first husband, Wes, to celebrate his sixty-fifth birthday along with several of his friends and colleagues. He and his field assistant, Judy Fierstein, had done field research and mapping of the huge Novarupta Crater over many summer seasons, and had published a lengthy research paper for the United States Geological Survey for whom they worked. Our group met in Anchorage and were flown by two ten-seater seaplanes to Brooks Lodge where Wes had reserved us all cabins. The flight took us over remote glaciers and valleys that are only accessible by pontoon planes that land on lakes or inlets.

After leaving Anchorage, our pilot said that if any of us needed to drop down onto a lake for a bathroom break to let him know. When we did make the request, he landed and said, "Do you want to pee from the pontoons or the shore?" Well, pontoons were fine for the men, but Debbie Mills and I said, "Take us to shore!" We were so desperate by this time, we just squatted on the beach with our raincoats around us. While I was peeing, I looked down to see huge grizzly tracks in the beach sand. We were in tundra, with no trees or cover, but luckily no bears in sight either. Back on board, we continued our trip with the pilot seeming uncertain where he was. Finally, we heard him on the radio with the other plane's pilot who said, "What are you doing way out there?" The plane had been built in 1961, the year I had graduated from high school, which made it about fifty years old at the time.

Eventually, much to our relief, we finally landed near the Katmai National Park headquarters and climbed out over the pontoons onto a beach. We knew we were in serious grizzly bear country when we were herded into a building, fresh off the plane, to have a bear-safety talk. Sure enough, over the next few days, we saw grizzlies ambling through the compound outside our cabins and the dining room. It barely got dark at night in August, so we never had to have bear encounters in the dark, but even in the light it was scary enough. Brooks Lodge is known for its accessible bear viewing, so part of our visit was to take a long group hike through the woods to a bear-viewing platform above the river; here we saw bears in the river fishing for salmon. Everywhere you walked in this country, you repeatedly said out loud in a big voice, "Hi, bear! Hey, bear!"

One day we traveled by tour bus to the Novarupta Crater overlook manned by National Park Service rangers and naturalists. From this area, we also descended into the crater by trail to where we could see the old ash flows close up. The whole experience was fascinating and new to all of us. Wes and his assistant, Judy, gave us an excellent tour. We enjoyed the hikes and the science with the camaraderie of old and new friends, most from Mill Valley or Berkeley. Someone made Wes a volcano cake, and he was clearly touched by comments and gifts, including a small photo book I gave him that included snapshots of him when he was younger.

When Roger and I left, we traveled by plane again with Deb and Scott Mills to Kodiak Island. On this flight, we had a well-known pilot named Sonny, who was honest in saying that the weather was difficult and he "would try" but couldn't guarantee we would make it without having to reroute back to Anchorage. We made it, however, by flying very low, under the clouds and through mountain passes, and I remember singing a Willie Nelson song, "Angel, Flying Too Close to the Ground." Our purpose for going to Kodiak Island was that Scott was to be interviewed about his relatives who had lived there during the Novarupta eruption in 1917. We landed on a lake, took a taxi, and were treated to a fancy Russian tea at a wonderful museum where Scott was interviewed as we all looked at the exhibits. We stayed the night in a motel, wandered the streets of Kodiak, found one restaurant with beer, and flew back to Anchorage the next morning to catch our plane home. It had been a wonderful, adventurous trip with friends.

We have also attended other major birthday events hosted by Wes to show us his field areas at Mount Adams, Washington, and Mammoth Lakes, California. In August 2018, his wife Gail hosted a wonderful eightieth celebration for him at their wooded second home among the redwoods in Felton, California. At each of these celebrations, we have gathered with old Mill Valley friends and geology colleagues. We are a mixed group including artists, writers, photographers, geologists, but all with a common interest in the outdoor world.

One of our favorite trips occurred at the suggestion of our good friends Stan and Judy Cooper from Mill Valley. Stan had grown up in Sturgis, South Dakota, and they still had a family home to which they traveled almost yearly. One of those years, in September 2001, ten days after 9/11, Roger and I left on a trip to drive the Wyoming section of the Mormon Pioneer Trail wherever it came near a road. Stan and Judy had given us a National Park Service map that highlighted all the major points, such as river crossings, South Pass, Forts Bridger and Laramie, Independence Rock, and sites where we could see wagon ruts. They also added their favorite place to buy huge ice cream cones in Farson, Wyoming. We traveled in our small twenty-two-foot motorhome and stayed along the way, either in parks or places that people offered us—one time behind an art gallery with deer grazing near a beautiful creek.

When we got to Sturgis, Stan and Judy toured us all through the Black Hills—took us to Deadwood where we sat in the bar where Buffalo Bill had been shot, and went up the hill where we visited the graves of Wild Bill and Calamity Jane. Then we visited the Thompson ranch where Stan and Judy's friend, Ed, showed us cattle and a few of the ten thousand acres. We had a cozy lunch there with Ed's ninety-three-year old mother, Lois, who gave Judy and me hand-crocheted pot holders. Everywhere the fall colors were spectacular—aspen, box elder, and sumac in bright colors. After a wonderful visit, we drove many scenic miles home. It was very touching that everywhere we traveled in the rural countryside, we saw American flags on fences, gates, and farm equipment, already commemorating those who had been killed. The country was deeply touched and in mourning that September.

For many years Roger and I traveled to Colorado to visit our friend Bob Krear, who lived in Estes Park next to Rocky Mountain National Park. I had known Bob from the days when I had lived in Death Valley with Wes. I learned a lot from him over the years, and we remained friends. Roger and he became good friends also, and we visited him every two or three years, welcomed as guests in his mountain house. We had to clear a few cobwebs from our basement room, but Bob was an excellent cook and host, and only allowed me to cook when he was in his nineties. When visiting Bob in autumn, Roger and I would be toured around in the evening to see the elk in rut either in the park or on the nearby golf course. They also wandered freely through the streets in downtown Estes Park, grazing on the landscaping at the library and other yummy sites.

Visiting Bob over the years was always very special. He aged gracefully, and though he became very hunched over from arthritis, he kept his mind active by reading books and research papers and watching many nature programs. He also swam at a public pool where they called him Charles Atlas because he was so fit in his old age. He had such interesting stories to tell from his young days as a wildlife researcher in Colorado and the Arctic with Olaus and Mardy Murie, who were instrumental in doing the research leading into the establishment of the Arctic National Wildlife Refuge. Because of Bob's connection with that research trip in the 1950s, he was invited to be a featured speaker as part of the celebration of the fiftieth anniversary of the establishment of ANWR. He invited us to accompany him and stay as his guests at the Murie Ranch in Moose, Wyoming. I had heard about the Muries for many years, and Roger and I were honored to be included in a weekend gathering of scientists and artists from various parts of the country. Bob continued to live in his cabin in Estes Park until he passed away at home on December 16, 2017, at the age of ninety-five. He had close friends who had been looking in on him often, and he was found in his bed where he died in his sleep. I had talked to him two weeks earlier, and I will miss hearing his familiar strong, deep voice.

As I near the end of my story, Roger is eighty-two and still riding Buddy, even after three joint replacements. I call him the Bionic Man. With all of Roger's patience and skill over the years, Buddy has become a wonderful horse. With him, Roger has joined the Alameda Country Volunteer Mounted Posse and rides in parades or events where they need help and representation. Recently, he rode in the first cattle drive at the Alameda County Fair, down the main street of Pleasanton. He also is a member of the East Bay Volunteer Mounted Patrol and scouts trails or attends events such as wildflower festivals, Cub Scout campouts, and fishing derbies for kids held in the parks. When not riding and caring for horses, Roger continues maintenance on our home, applying all those talents of electrician, plumber, and carpenter that are rare in one person these days.

For many years I have enjoyed greeting the sunrise on a walk each day, though currently the walk is short because I am recovering from recent knee replacement. I've covered a lot of trails in my life, so it's not surprising that my knees are wearing out, but I plan to hike again when I am fully recovered. I probably won't ride anymore, but my small mule, Taco, hollers for his meals twice a day, and he is a very obedient companion when my grandchildren lead him around the property. I miss Georgia, but when she developed arthritis, I gave her to a mule man who rides her on his forty-acre flat ranch in Northern California.

Every day we enjoy watching our horses in pasture out our kitchen window, and our porch cats, who appeared four years ago, are eating us out of house and home. Often on summer evenings, we sit on our back porch with them and look east at the alpenglow on the golden, rolling hills, and we comment on how lucky we are. Sometimes we visit with neighbors, Bobbie Meyer and Marilyn and Jerry Russell. We call ourselves "the fivesome" and take turns hosting dinners at our country homes. There never seems to be a lack of things to talk about—everything from wildlife sightings and fence disputes to politics and the good books we all enjoy.

On my seventy-fifth birthday in March 2018, Alison and Mitch threw a large party at their house on the Stanford campus. It was a festive event with good food and folk singing with friends from all stages of my life. Included in this group were high school friends also turning seventy-five, Suzy McCulloch and Nancy Piver on ukulele. With my reflective nature, I had imagined myself quietly celebrating on the shore of a mountain lake or desert sand dune and wasn't sure I wanted a party, but I now realize how special it was to be honored at this milestone.

Going forward, there are still many things I want to do in this life. I will hike in the mountains as long as I am able. Also, I have resumed my love of music with piano lessons and guitar. The weeds in the garden call to me, as well as piles of books I want to read. I still have Roger's steady love and companionship, and I am fortunate to have such a loving family and lifelong friendships. I am also thankful that, by writing this memoir, I have been able to recall so many special people and parts of my life. Like any life, there have been bumps in the road and forks in the trail, but I've always been able to reflect, dig deep, and move forward. I look ahead to many more years with my family and having thoughtful, quiet time in nature wherever my feet will take me.

Roger, Nancy, and Ben

Roger Brown

Roger and Nancy on Wheeler Peak, Nevada, 1993

Roger and Buddy

Alison ready for whitewater canoeing

Roger and Ben on the Missouri River

Nancy on her mule Georgia

Roger in Capitol Reef National Park, Utah

Roger with first grandchild, Miles, 2005

Nancy with Isaac, Eliza, Jada, and Miles, 2008

Isaac, Jada, Eliza, and Miles

Rocky, Buddy, Roger, Jake, Taco, Nancy, and Georgia (photo by Jean Schreiber)

Valerie, Roger, Cameron, 2018

Isaac, Eliza, and Ana, 2017

Eliza, Alison, Isaac, and Mitchell, Palo Alto, California, 2016

Acknowledgments

This memoir comes from a life well lived. I never could have predicted all the forks in the road and all the people who have enriched my life, but looking back, I see there are many to thank for making my life adventurous and meaningful. With sincere gratitude, I thank the following people:

Roger Brown, my best friend and devoted husband of nearly thirty years, both adventurer and family man who sits in the saddle as well as he hikes.

Alison Marsden, my beautiful and talented daughter, who is a master at balancing academic life with family and adventure.

Jerry Marsden, for being a loving father to Alison, missed by all who knew him. And to his Canadian relatives still in our lives.

Mitchell Mutz, the best son-in-law a mother could have and the best cook.

Eliza and Isaac Mutz, Miles and Jada Morris, beloved grandchildren and hikers, musicians, artists, scientists, and authors of the future.

Valerie Thomey and Cameron Casey, stepdaughter and stepson, for spirit and tie-dye, photos and love.

Sheri Morris, always a loving member of the family—and appreciation of our jokes about whether "the doctor is in."

Wes Hildreth, for carrying the first backpack and taking us to national parks and peaks I never would have dreamed I could climb.

Suzy Rosse McCulloch and Nancy Piver for all the adventures growing up and the art and music going forward.

Lauren Williams, my talented brother, "Larry," who remembers it all and helped me recall family history.

Lubov Mazur for spirit and friendship for more than forty years. And for Michael, whose gentle nature and humor are never forgotten.

Sugie Barker, a writer herself and dear mountain friend, for nudging me to keep writing this memoir. John Barker for hikes, friendship, and mountain stories. Thanks to both for sharing the mountains at Elwell Lodge.

Mayme Hubert, my new, supportive writing friend.

Alzak Amlani, for his wisdom and talent in helping me find my inner spirit and ability to tell this story.

Mill Valley friends George and Marti Cagwin, Ralph Brott, Deb and Scott Mills, Stan and Judy Cooper, Judy Marvin, Jack and Diane Fulton, for all the picnics, hikes, songs, and parties.

Livermore neighbors Bobbie Meyer and Marilyn and Jerry Russell for lasting friendship and enthusiastic conversation over dinner and on the trails.

Molly Giles, short story writer, for excellent, insightful editing of my first draft and helping me see I could publish this memoir.

Editors of iUniverse for caring help and steady communication for a new writer.

Lastly, the Sleeping Maiden of Mount Tamalpais for a lifetime of inspiration.

About the Author

NANCY W. BROWN is a California native who spent her youth camping, hiking, and fishing with her family. As an adult, she has backpacked, lived in national parks, canoed rivers, and ridden her mule on mountain and desert trails. She earned a teaching credential, bachelor of arts, and master of arts from University of California, Berkeley. She is retired from teaching and lives with her husband on a horse ranch in Livermore, California.

Printed in the United States
By Bookmasters